# THE DOLLS NEED HELP.

"You all know about the war," Papa begins. "Well, even though America is not fighting, the war will still affect us here."

"How, Papa?" I ask.

"Doll parts," he says. "The parts we use come from Germany. And because of the war, we won't be able to get them. Not for a long time, anyway."

"Why not?" asks Trudie.

"Because America is going to stop trading with Germany. That's what happens when countries go to war. Everything suffers."

There is a long, heavy silence while we try to make sense of what he has just said.

"How can you fix the dolls without the parts, Papa?" Trudie finally asks.

"I can't," says Papa. "At least, I can't repair any dolls whose parts I don't have here already."

"If you and Mama can't fix dolls, what will happen to the shop? And what will happen to us?" asks Sophie. Those are the exact questions I want to ask, but I am afraid to hear the answers.

"I'm not sure," Papa says again, looking down at his hands as if he doesn't quite know what to do with them anymore.

# OTHER BOOKS YOU MAY ENJOY

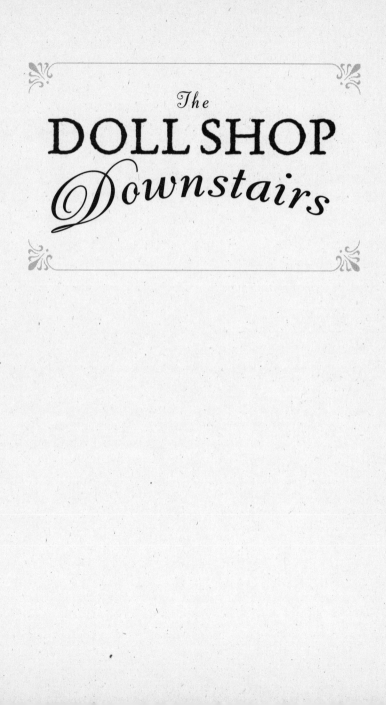

The
# DOLL SHOP
*Downstairs*

# The
# DOLL SHOP
## Downstairs

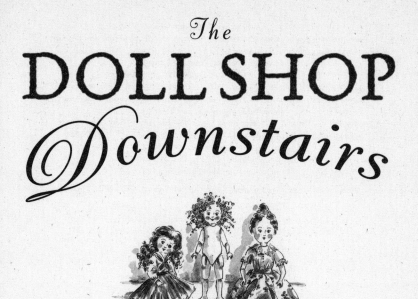

*by*

## YONA ZELDIS MCDONOUGH

*illustrated by*

## HEATHER MAIONE

**PUFFIN BOOKS**
An Imprint of Penguin Group (USA) Inc.

PUFFIN BOOKS

Published by the Penguin Group

Penguin Young Readers Group, 345 Hudson Street, New York, New York 10014, U.S.A.

Penguin Group (Canada), 90 Eglinton Avenue East, Suite 700, Toronto, Ontario, Canada M4P 2Y3
(a division of Pearson Penguin Canada Inc.)

Penguin Books Ltd, 80 Strand, London WC2R 0RL, England

Penguin Ireland, 25 St Stephen's Green, Dublin 2, Ireland (a division of Penguin Books Ltd)

Penguin Group (Australia), 250 Camberwell Road, Camberwell, Victoria 3124, Australia
(a division of Pearson Australia Group Pty Ltd)

Penguin Books India Pvt Ltd, 11 Community Centre, Panchsheel Park, New Delhi - 110 017, India

Penguin Group (NZ), 67 Apollo Drive, Rosedale, Auckland 0632, New Zealand
(a division of Pearson New Zealand Ltd)

Penguin Books (South Africa) (Pty) Ltd, 24 Sturdee Avenue,
Rosebank, Johannesburg 2196, South Africa

Registered Offices: Penguin Books Ltd, 80 Strand, London WC2R 0RL, England

First published in the United States of America by Viking,
a division of Penguin Young Readers Group, 2009
Published by Puffin Books, a division of Penguin Young Readers Group, 2011

1 3 5 7 9 10 8 6 4 2

THE LIBRARY OF CONGRESS HAS CATALOGED THE VIKING EDITION AS FOLLOWS:

McDonough, Yona Zeldis.

The doll shop downstairs / by Yona Zeldis McDonough ; illustrated by Heather Maione.

p. cm.

Summary: When World War I breaks out, nine-year-old Anna thinks of a way to save
her family's beloved New York City doll repair shop. Includes brief author's note about
the history of the Madame Alexander doll, a glossary, and timeline.

ISBN: 978-0-670-01091-2 (hc)

[1. Dolls—Fiction. 2. Dolls—Repairing—Fiction. 3. Family life—New York (State)—New York—
Fiction. 4. Immigrants—New York (State)—New York—Fiction. 5. Jews—United States—Fiction.
6. New York (N.Y.)—History—1898–1951—Fiction.]

I. Maione, Heather Harms, ill. II. Title

PZ7.M15655Du 2009

[Fic]—dc22   2009001934

Puffin Books ISBN 978-0-14-241691-4

Book design by Nancy Brennan
Set in Kennerley

Printed in the United States of America

*For Joy Peskin, who believed in the magic
of the doll shop from the very start.*

*My thanks to Regina Hayes and Nancy Brennan for
their support and their faith, and to Janet Pascal
for her meticulous research and invaluable suggestions.
Thanks, too, to Leon Thurm for his formidable memory.*—Y.Z.M.

*To my mamish, with love.*—H.M.

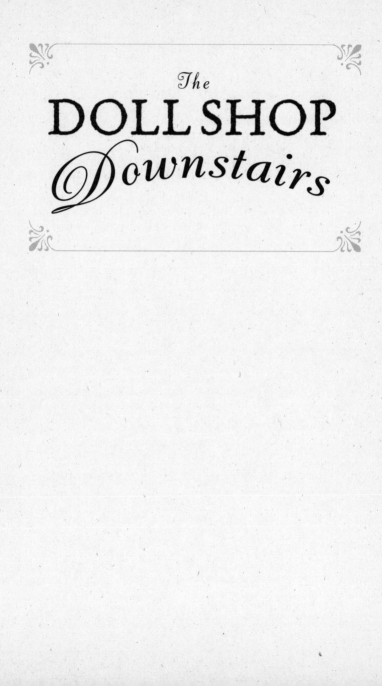

# The
# DOLL SHOP
## Downstairs

# I

## MEET THE DOLLS

"Don't push!" I tell my little sister, Trudie.

"I'm not pushing, Anna," says Trudie. "You are!"

"If you two fight, Mama will make us go back upstairs," says our big sister, Sophie. Sophie is eleven, but right now she is talking to us like she is a grown-up and we are just babies. Well, maybe she thinks Trudie is a baby, but *I'm* not, so I wish she would stop using that tone.

Sophie, Trudie, and I have spent most of the afternoon cleaning the doll repair shop our parents own and run. Now we are allowed to stay in the shop to play. But Sophie is right: if we quarrel, Mama will hear us and make us come upstairs. So I let Trudie go ahead, even if she does shove her way in front of me and step on my foot besides. Trudie *is* only seven so I suppose I should be understanding.

I've always lived above the doll shop on Essex Street. Mama says that a long time ago, when Sophie was a baby, the three of them lived in a different apartment, on Ludlow Street. But to me, Ludlow Street doesn't count. It's Essex Street, and only Essex Street, that is home. Out in front there is a sign that reads:

## BREITTLEMANN'S DOLL REPAIR
### All Kinds of Dolls Lovingly Restored and Mended
*Established 1904*

Underneath the letters is a picture of a smiling doll. Mama painted it. She can paint a picture of anything. She is the one who paints the dolls' faces—the rosy cheeks, the red lips—so well that you'd never know they weren't brand new. I tell her I think she is a magician, but she only smiles and keeps her hand steady on the brush.

Trudie runs ahead of me and reaches for "her" doll, which is made of bisque and has thick, dark hair. The doll is not really hers, of course. All the dolls here are waiting to be fixed by Papa. But while they wait, he

lets us play with them. We each choose a single doll at a time—that's the rule—and we have to be careful when we play. The dolls are very fragile and easy to break. The only time a doll can leave the shop is with its owner. We are not owners. We have no bisque or china dolls that belong to just us. Bisque and china dolls are expensive. We used to have rag dolls that Mama made, but they have fallen apart from so much use, and she has not had a chance to make new ones. Papa says that if the shop does really, really well, one day he will buy each of us a doll of our own. But it seems to me that day is a long way off.

"Angelica Grace!" breathes Trudie when she sees her doll. Angelica Grace is a name Sophie came up with. She read it in a book and told it to Trudie. Sophie comes up with all the names for our dolls—she's good at that, but then, she is good at so many things.

Compared to some of the other dolls in the shop, Angelica Grace doesn't look too bad. Her navy pleated skirt and white sailor blouse are only a little wrinkled. Her hair is neat. She even has navy leather shoes and white ribbed stockings on her feet. But one of her blue glass eyes is missing, and there is a big, dark hole where it once was. It makes her look kind of spooky.

Sophie's current doll—she calls her Victoria Marie— looks much worse. The toes of her bare feet are broken, and her blonde hair is always tangled, though Sophie tries to comb it. All of her clothes are missing. But she has the sweetest smile, and tiny holes in her earlobes where real earrings can fit.

The doll that is "mine" is Bernadette Louise. Her face, legs, and arms are made of shiny glazed porcelain. Her dark hair is painted on and decorated with beautiful painted blue flowers. Mama says they are morning glo- ries. On one foot, she wears a black painted boot with a blue tassled garter; the other foot is missing. Her dark red and gold flowered skirt must have been nice once, but it is now torn and stained. Her right arm is badly cracked.

One day, I asked Papa why these three dolls were still in the shop. Usually he mends the dolls promptly and then sends them home again.

"Which dolls?" he asked, and I showed him the three dolls we thought of as "ours."

"I'm having trouble getting the right color eye for this doll," Papa said, pointing to Angelica Grace. "The blues I find are always wrong." He frowned slightly. "But I keep trying. One day, I'll find an eye that's a perfect match."

"And the others?"

"Well, the owners of this doll," he said, looking at Victoria Marie, "told me they were going on a long trip. No one will be able to pick the doll up for quite a while so there's no rush in fixing her." He smoothed the doll's tangled hair gently. "Now this doll," he said, picking up Bernadette Louise and looking into her face, "is very old—much older than the other two. Getting the right parts for her has been very difficult. They don't make legs or arms the way they used to; I keep hoping I'll find the perfect ones. But so far, I haven't."

Sometimes, Papa can fix a broken part with his file or one of his other tools. But when he can't fix a part, he has to get a new one. He orders them all the way from Germany, where most of the dolls are made. The doll parts arrive in huge boxes brought by the postman, Mr. Greevy.

Sophie, Trudie, and I are always thrilled when a box arrives, and if we are not in school, we stop whatever we are doing to help Papa open and sort through it. Inside, there are doll arms and legs of different sizes and shapes, all packed in straw and shredded paper. There are lots of wigs—blonde, brown, red, black; braids, buns, curls. Doll bodies are in the box, too, and sometimes clothes. Even though Mama could make or repair anything, a customer sometimes requests a special outfit. Once we found a doll-sized fancy gray silk ball gown and matching evening coat. Another time, there was a satin bridal dress with a train, veil, and the most adorable tiny white leather gloves.

But the very best things in the box are the glass eyes. Because they are so fragile, the eyes are packed first in tissue, then straw, and then finally in their own tiny boxes. Each glass eye is a hollow white ball with a different color in the center. Some are dark, inky blue, while others are sky blue, chocolate brown, amber, or green.

"I wish our dolls had a bed," says Trudie now, the whine just beginning to creep into her voice. Sophie, who has found Victoria Marie and is busy trying to smooth out her hair, ignores her. "We need a bed." Now Trudie really is whining.

I want to shake her. But if I do, I will get in trouble with Mama. So instead, I say, "Guess what? We *have* a bed."

"We do?" Trudie asks, eyes wide. Even Sophie looks interested. "Where is it?"

"Right here!" I say, and drag something out from behind the glass-topped counter.

"Oh!" breathes Trudie when she sees it. Of course, if you didn't know, the thing I dragged out might not look much like a bed at all, and instead might seem to be an ordinary wooden box. In fact, it is a box, given to me by Mr. Bloom, who owns the grocery shop on the corner. The box originally held vegetables but now that it was empty, Mr. Bloom was happy to give it to me. Made of smooth golden wood, the box is deep and sturdy. As soon as I saw it, I knew it was a perfect place for three dolls to spend the night.

"That was a good idea, Anna," Sophie says. I stand up a little straighter when she says that. Even though Sophie can annoy me by being so very perfect, her praise still matters. She doesn't give me much of it, either.

"Go ahead, put her in," urges Sophie, and Trudie places her doll in the bottom of the box. Sophie and I do the same. Then Trudie bursts out, "But we don't have a blanket! How can they sleep without a blanket?"

"You don't have to cry," says Sophie. "I have a blanket."

"Where? Where is it? I want to see!" says Trudie. I'm curious, too. What does Sophie have in mind?

"Here," Sophie says, and she pulls something white and soft from the pocket of her apron.

"A pillow case!" says Trudie. "How perfect!" She gazes up adoringly at Sophie. "You always know how to fix things," she adds. Somehow, this makes me feel cross. Trudie didn't get all *that* excited over the bed that I found for us; it's always Sophie this, Sophie that, Sophie, Sophie, Sophie.

"Where did you get it?" I ask.

"From Mama's rag basket," says Sophie.

Then she tucks the pillowcase up around the dolls' chins.

"Will she mind?"

"No, silly! It's a rag." Sophie uses that superior, I'm-so-grown-up voice again.

"Can we leave them in the box all night?" asks Trudie, sounding worried.

"Yes," says Sophie. "They'll be safe. I promise."

"Good night, Angelica Grace," says Trudie. She leans over to kiss her doll, loudly, on the cheek.

"Good night," says Sophie to her own doll as she and Trudie head for the stairs. "Are you coming?" she asks me. Even though she has put the light out, I can feel her looking at me.

"In a minute," I tell her.

She doesn't say anything else but just takes Trudie's hand and goes upstairs.

I listen to their footsteps as they go, but I don't follow them right away. I want to be alone down here for a little bit. Sometimes it's hard being a middle sister, and I just need to be by myself. Sophie is smart and pretty and good at so many things; Trudie (her real name is Gertrude, though we never call her that) is little and cute and cries to get her way. I'm just the one sort of stuffed in between—at nine I'm not old enough to do some things, like light the kitchen stove, but too old to do others, like snuggle in Mama and Papa's bed on a cold morning.

I can hear the sounds of my family moving around above me. In a minute, I know Mama will be calling me to come up. There is a narrow stairway leading up to our apartment, which has four small rooms. Mama does her best to keep our home cheerful and comfortable. "It may not be fancy," she likes to say, "but it can still be fine."

She painted our kitchen a color she calls Persian blue, and she grows red geraniums in wooden window boxes. She calls them her "windowsill garden." In the center of the room is a big table where we eat, and after the dishes are cleared, we do our lessons. The parlor, which is pale peach, has a small settee and two armchairs. Mama keeps a standing lamp between the chairs, so that in the evenings, Papa can read his paper while she does her sewing. Mama and Papa's bedroom is painted mint green. Mama crocheted a white coverlet for the bed, and she made lace trim for the muslin curtains that hang in the windows. The room Sophie, Trudie, and I share is pale pink. The color looks like the inside of a seashell. The apartment has only one sink, which is in the kitchen, and the bathtub is there, too, covered by a hinged white wooden top that can be raised when the tub is in use and lowered when it isn't. Papa designed and made that. The toilet is out in the hall and we have to share it.

I like our apartment, even if it is kind of small. And I love the doll shop. Because I love it, I almost never mind helping with the weekly cleaning. Sophie, Trudie, and I take turns sweeping, wiping the counters and shelves, and polishing the big plate-glass window and the counter-top with a rag dipped in sudsy ammonia water. Then we each have our own special chore: Sophie organizes the doll parts, Trudie dusts the dolls with a big feather duster, and I am in charge of the birdcage. Papa has a canary for company while he works, and I am the one to keep the cage fresh and tidy. The canary is named Goldie, because of his color, and he sings all day long. At night, I usually put an old dish towel over the cage, but today I forgot. When I make my way over to the cage in the dark, I see Goldie hopping back and forth from one perch to another.

"Are you lonely down here by yourself?" I ask him. Goldie stops and cocks his little head, as if he is listening to me. Then he starts hopping again. I pick up the dish towel and cover the cage. I look over at my doll, which is snuggled in the box-that-is-a-bed with the other dolls. "You can keep him company," I tell Bernadette Louise. And somehow, I know she will.

# 2

## SCHOOL DAYS

The next few days are very busy, and we have no time to play in the doll shop. Sophie and I both have arithmetic examinations at school. For me, that means I must work extra hard. I enjoy some of my lessons, like reading. Even though I'm two years younger than Sophie, I can read almost all the books she can. And I'm good at history and geography, too. I can easily memorize the names of all the presidents and the state capitals. But arithmetic makes my head pound and my palms sweat. When I see a whole page of figures I have to add or subtract, I feel like I can't breathe. Multiplication is even worse. I practice the times tables at breakfast, on the way to school, while I am getting ready for bed. "Seven times seven is forty-nine," I say softly. "Seven times eight is fifty-six. . . ." But they are still all fuzzy in my mind.

Coming home from school on Wednesday—the day before the examinations—I tell Sophie I am worried. She seems impatient. "Well, you just have to memorize the times tables."

"I know." I wish she could be a little more sympathetic. "I'm trying."

"You'd better try harder," is Sophie's reply. "You don't want to get a D, do you?"

"Of course not," I say. What I do not say is that I am afraid I will get an F, not even a D.

Trudie picks up on my fear and starts teasing me—"Anna's getting an F, Anna's getting an F"—which makes me feel even worse.

But though I am worried about the examination, I don't want to tell Mama and Papa; they have enough to think about right now. Although it's early April, the weather has been blustery, and Papa has come down with a bad cold. Now he's behind with his repair work in the shop. We have to help out with some of Mama's chores upstairs, while Mama does what she can with the doll repair. I have been washing the dishes, changing the sheets, and sweeping the floor, along with trying to memorize those miserable times tables.

On Thursday morning, I pick at my pumpernickel bread and jam; everyone else is too busy to even notice that I hardly eat a thing. Sophie and Trudie walk ahead of me on the way to school. I lag behind, not at all eager to arrive. Here's Guttman's Pickle Shop, where Mama gets the crunchy pickles we all love; there's Zeitlin's Bakery, where they make the most delicious cinnamon buns. Down one street is the *shul* where we all go for services on Saturdays; down another is an empty lot where we sometimes play when the weather is warm. Other kids from the neighborhood join us: we play tag and stickball, and we jump rope. I wish I could go there now. In fact, I wish I could go anywhere other than where I am going now.

When I eventually get to school, my sisters are nowhere to be seen. Sophie must have gone up to her sixth-grade classroom. Trudie is in the second grade. I slip into my seat in fourth grade just seconds before we are about to start the day. I'm lucky the teacher, Miss Morrison, is busy at her desk and doesn't mark me late. Three late marks and you have to stay after school. I already have two.

Quickly I unpack my books into my desk. Then I stand with my hand over my heart when it is time to say the Pledge of Allegiance. Miss Morrison hands out paper and tells us to take out our pencils. I tremble a little when she calls out, "Nine times seven," but then I take some deep breaths to calm myself and think, hard, about what the answer is—sixty-three. Soon the examination is over. What a relief! When it's time for recess in the yard, I run and skip with Batya and Esther, my two best friends in class. At lunch, I take out the brown paper bag Mama has packed for me: rye bread spread with horseradish, a cold boiled potato, and an apple. I won't know what I got on the examination until tomorrow, so I don't have to worry about it until then. When we get home, we find that Papa is feeling better and is back at work in the shop. We are all grateful for that.

The next day, I get my examination back. There is a big red "B" on the top of the paper. B is not a bad grade, especially when I thought I might get an F. That night, when we welcome Shabbos together, everyone seems happy, like it is a party. Mama makes brisket with carrots and onions, and for dessert, there is spice cake.

<hr />

Saturday is our day of rest. We don't work in the shop or at home. Instead, we put on our best dresses—Mama made these, too—and together we walk to *shul*. While Mama and Papa go upstairs, Sophie, Trudie, and I head downstairs to the children's service that is led by Miss Epstein. She reads from a big book with beautiful color illustrations: Noah and the ark, Jacob and the angel, Rebecca at the well. I like the stories so much that Miss Epstein lets me look at the book by myself when the service is over and the other children are playing.

On the way home, it starts to pour. No one thought to bring an umbrella, so we have to hurry. Even so, we still get soaked. At home, I have to squeeze water out of my stockings and stuff crumpled balls of newspaper in my shoes so they won't lose their shape.

After lunch, I feel bored and restless. Usually we take a walk on Shabbos. I like seeing the streets—usually so noisy, so crowded—quiet and still. Once, I saw a cat with her newborn kittens inside a doorway; another time, I found a broken locket in the shape of a heart glinting up at me from the gray cobblestones. If it had been a normal busy day, I never would have noticed it.

Today, though, is not a day for a walk. The rain hits the windows with a sound like pebbles being tossed, and I can hear the noise of the wind as it blows. This is a day for staying inside. A day for the doll shop. I go and look for my parents. Papa is having a nap. Mama is in her chair, darning socks. I ask her if we can go down to play. Maybe even have a tea party.

"A tea party? For the dolls?" asks Mama. Sophie and I both look at her. Will she agree? "You've all worked so hard this week," Mama says. "I think you girls could have a little party today."

So after Mama helps us gather what we will need, we all head down to the doll shop. This time, I don't even try to get ahead of Trudie but just let her go first. She rushes to the box-that-is-a-bed and takes out her doll. Sophie follows her, but I stop to take the cover off Goldie's cage. "Hello, little fellow," I say to him. Does he understand me? Probably not, but he hops along his perch so happily that I can't help believing he is glad to see us. I take my doll and bring her close to Goldie, so he can see her, too.

Sophie flips the box over and covers it with the pillow-case. "There's the table," she says, "and the tablecloth." I have to admit, Sophie can be very clever. She's also pretty, with straight, shiny brown hair that stays neatly braided. Not like mine, which is thick and wild and is always a bit of a mess.

Next we set the table with three old saucers Mama no longer uses. The saucers are chipped, but they have a pretty pattern of grapes around the borders. There are no proper cups, but Mama offers me a thimble for Bernadette Louise, who is the smallest of the dolls. For the other two, she gives us small tin measuring cups. The smallest ones, one-eighth, are just the right size. And maybe they'll help me with fractions, I think, hold-ing one in my hand. I know fractions are coming soon, and I am dreading them.

Mama also gives us a small glass saltcellar. "That can

be the centerpiece," she says. And when she brings the sweetened tea down to pour, she brings a small box of animal crackers, too.

"Look at those!" exclaims Trudie, delighted by the lion-, giraffe-, and hippopotamus-shaped cookies.

Mama puts the cookies on the plates and lets Sophie pour the tea before she goes upstairs. The tea is cold; Mama made it yesterday. We can't light a fire because lighting a fire is considered work, and we are not supposed to work on Shabbos, which lasts from Friday evening to Saturday night. But the tea is good anyway, strong and sweet. The saltcellar shines like crystal on the white tablecloth. "There are no chairs," says Trudie. It sounds like she might start to cry.

"We'll be the chairs then," says Sophie quickly.

"What do you mean?" Trudie asks.

"Let's each take our doll and put her on our lap. That way she can eat and drink comfortably."

"Oh yes!" cries Trudie.

"Do you like tea?" I ask Bernadette Louise. I don't really expect a reply, but it does seem that she has a special, contented look on her face that means, "Yes, I do like tea."

Sitting here in the shop with my sisters and the dolls, I find myself thinking about what happened when Sophie brought home *her* arithmetic exam with a big red A on the first page. I was so jealous of the fuss Mama and Papa made. You'd think no one in the world had ever gotten an A before. It made my B seem, oh, I don't know—shabby somehow.

But right now, even that disappointment seems to fade. After we finish our tea and cookies, we pretend that my doll, Bernadette Louise, is getting married. Sophie pins the pillowcase around her to make a wedding dress; Angelica Grace and Victoria Marie are the bridesmaids. Later, I offer to stay downstairs and clean up by myself. Sophie and Trudie think I am being nice, but the truth is that I want to be alone so I can tell Bernadette Louise all about my week: the worry about the examination, Trudie's teasing, Sophie's lack of sympathy, my own jealousy because Sophie did better than me. I don't actually talk out loud to her; I don't have to. I pretend she understands what I'm thinking as well as what I'm saying. Sometimes I don't know how or why this comforts me. But it does.

# 3

## HAPPY BIRTHDAY

Spring is birthday season in our family. Trudie's comes first, on April 30. Mine is a few weeks later, on May 15, and Sophie's is just three days after that.

"My pretty spring flowers," says Mama. "We'll have to think of a birthday treat." I know that there isn't money for a big party or lots of fancy presents. Still, Mama and Papa always try to make the occasion special. Last year, we brought a picnic to Central Park, all the way uptown. Mama spread a big blanket on the grass, and we had sandwiches, cold tea, and fruit, and for dessert, Papa pulled foil-wrapped chocolate coins from his pocket. This year, Mama says we can do the same thing, but adds something new.

"How would you girls like to visit F.A.O. Schwartz?"

I am not sure what F.A.O. Schwartz is, but before I can ask, Sophie says, "F.A.O. Schwartz? The big toy store on Fifth Avenue?" Sophie, as I've said, knows so many things.

"Yes." Mama nods. "Our shop has been doing well, so Papa and I thought each of you could pick out a small present."

"A present! From the toy store!" Trudie begins to sing the words, and adds a little dance. "A present! A present!"

"It will have to be a very small one," Mama says. "We don't have money to buy you each a doll. But something small, maybe something dolls could use, would be all right."

"You mean like clothes?" I say.

"Yes," Mama agrees. "That's a good idea. "We'll go to the store first, and then we can walk up to Central Park for our picnic."

"A present! A picnic!" sings Trudie. She is so excited. And so am I.

On a Monday in late May, there is a school holiday. That's the day Papa chooses for our picnic. He'll close the shop early and we'll leave by noon. Of course it turns out to be the busiest day the store has had in a while. Goldie twitters and chirps madly from all the activity. First a man with bushy whiskers comes into the shop with a broken doll that he holds by the foot. He seems to be in an exceedingly bad mood.

"Children!" he fumes, setting the doll on the counter. "Always breaking something."

"Dolls are fragile," Papa says, examining the doll. "But don't worry, we can make her as good as new."

"When?" asks the man. It seems to me he is rude, but Papa speaks to him politely anyway.

"Next Thursday," says Papa. As he is writing up the ticket, a lady comes in. She is with a girl, a little younger than me, in a sky-blue linen dress. The girl's eyes are red-rimmed, like she's been crying; in her arms she clutches a great big baby doll with a cracked head.

"Do you think you can fix her?" the lady asks Papa when he is finished with the man. The girl stands shyly behind the lady, still clutching the doll.

"May I?" Papa asks the girl. He takes the doll and gently runs his fingers over her head. Then he looks at the girl. "I know I can," says Papa with a smile. She sniffs a bit, but she manages a small smile back at Papa.

Then two more people—a short man whose white hair is very thick and a lady wearing gold-rimmed spectacles—come into the shop. They are both carrying dolls that need mending. So many dolls that need Papa's and Mama's loving hands. What would they do without them?

Finally, the customers are gone and Papa is able to put a big sign on the door that says CLOSED. Mama has packed a lunch that Papa carries in a big straw basket. We walk to the Second Avenue El and climb the stairs that lead up to the platform. Papa buys us each a ticket, which we then drop into the chute of a big wooden ticket chopper. A man in a uniform and cap works a handle to chop up the tickets. Trudie is a little bit scared of the ticket chopper and doesn't want to go near it. But I reassure her that there is no way the chopper can grab her hand, and she finally is willing to drop her ticket in.

The shiny brown train comes almost right away and when the doors slide open, we step inside. The car is very new and smart looking; the floors are red and the seats are covered with wicker. When the train pulls out of the station, we girls are jolted a little bit and we laugh. "Hold on!" Papa tells us as we each grab a strap. "Hold on tight!"

We ride for about twenty minutes, and when we get off at Thirty-fourth Street, we are in a different world. We have left behind the packed, narrow streets of our neighborhood—Essex, Delancy, Orchard, Ludlow, Hester, and Rivington—that are crammed with shops, horses and wagons, pushcarts, and crowds of people. You can buy almost anything you want on those streets: poppy seeds and pocketknives, socks and soap flakes, buttons and bagels. And there are so many languages you might hear: Yiddish, German, Polish, Romanian, and Russian, sometimes all at once. Our parents are from Russia, so they speak Russian and Yiddish. They only learned English when they came to America, before any of us were born. Sometimes Mama and Papa speak Yiddish when they

don't want us to understand what they are saying.

But here we find wide streets, like Fifth Avenue, that are filled with fine shops selling silk parasols, evening gloves, and the most amazing hats I have ever seen. Some are decorated with fake fruits and flowers, or even, in one case, what looks like a real stuffed bird. And the people are so elegant here; they stroll rather than hurry and push the way they do downtown. I don't hear any Yiddish or Russian, only English. At least Mama and Papa know how to speak English, even if they have accents and sometimes forget a word or two and have to go fishing for it in another language. My friends Batya and Esther both have parents who speak only Yiddish.

I glance at Mama, whose clothes are not as expensive and well tailored as most of the other ladies who walk past. But no one else has Mama's perfect posture, or that special way of tilting her head when something she likes catches her eye. I feel proud of her, and even though I think it is sort of babyish, I slip my hand into hers as we walk. Mama smiles down at me.

Soon we come to the toy store at the corner of Fifth Avenue and Thirty-first Street. Inside, there are whole counters that contain nothing but dolls: big dolls and small dolls, baby dolls and grown-up lady dolls, dolls that come with a steamer trunk full of clothes or their very own doll-sized furniture.

"That doll has a canopy bed!" says Sophie. "Look at the ruffles on the bedspread."

"I've never seen so many dolls," says Trudie.

"They do have a huge selection," says Papa. And it's true.

Even sophisticated Sophie is impressed. She touches a tall, auburn-haired doll with a crimson gown and pearl tiara. "Maybe this one is a countess," she says. But Mama gently reminds us that there is probably nothing we can afford here, so we keep on looking. I am awed by the racks of doll dresses and all the accessories that go with them.

"What about this?" asks Trudie, holding up a doll-sized version of a lady's hand fan. "I think Angelica Grace would love it."

"Hmmm," says Sophie in a way that indicates this would not be her first choice.

As we wander, we stop often to touch what we see.

Mama and Papa do the same; dolls are their business after all, and it's good for them to see what F.A.O. Schwartz is selling.

We spend nearly an hour in the store, but no one can decide on anything. Trudie still likes the fan, though she is not sure—she would also like to get a hat for Angelica Grace. I am thinking about doll furniture, but I can't find anything we can afford. Sophie says she just has not found the right thing yet. Papa, who seems to have seen enough dolls for the moment, pulls out his newspaper and begins to read. Mama tells us we need to make a decision soon. Sophie is about to say something, but then she stops in front of a display we have somehow not seen before.

"Doll dishes," she says. I can hear the certainty in her voice.

"That's a good idea," says Mama. "You girls do love tea parties." So we gather around Sophie, inspecting first some plain white dishes and then a set of pots and pans.

"Here's a dolly rolling pin!" calls out Trudie. "Maybe they can bake."

Mama walks over to Sophie and hands her the box containing the white dishes. "This is not too expensive."

"I know, Mama. It's just kind of plain, that's all," says Sophie. I can tell she doesn't like it. Mama is about to speak again when Sophie's attention is caught by something else. "Look at this." She points to a different tea set—creamer, teapot, sugar bowl, four dainty cups, four saucers, and four dessert plates, all in the same deep yellow. Their color reminds me of Goldie, only darker. They come packed in a woven straw case with a bamboo handle. Inside there is a green and white checked lining and four green and white checked napkins. There are even four silver-plated spoons, knives, and forks, just the right size for doll hands.

"Can I get it, Mama?" Sophie asks shyly. Mama glances at the price tag and looks at Sophie. Papa rolls up his paper and comes over to see as well.

"I can understand why you want this set," Mama says slowly. "It's very, very lovely. But I think it's more than we can afford—"

"I have an idea," Sophie interrupts. "Mama, Papa, can we buy the tea set and have it be a present for all of us? Something we can share?"

They look at each other, thinking it over. "Well, we

have to ask your sisters," Papa points out. I touch the wicker case.

"It's a little picnic hamper," I say. "We could pretend the dolls are having a picnic."

"Then you say yes?" Sophie asks. She looks so hopeful. I nod. Then we both look at Trudie.

"I'm not sure," Trudie says. "I wanted to get the fan. Or a hat."

"This would be something we could all use together," I say. "It would be fun."

"But that fan . . ." says Trudie. There's the familiar whine creeping into her voice again.

"Well if Trudie doesn't say yes, then we can't buy it," Sophie says. She sounds annoyed.

"That's true," Mama says.

"You're so stubborn," says Sophie angrily. I'm surprised. Usually I'm the one to lose my temper with Trudie, not my oh-so-perfect big sister.

"Am not!" Trudie says angrily.

"Are too!" says Sophie. Her voice is loud, and a lady with a little boy turns to look.

"Sophie, please lower your voice," says Mama.

"Girls, you have to stop this right now," Papa says. He turns to Mama and adds, "Maybe a trip to the toy store wasn't such a good idea after all."

"Yes, it was. Only Trudie had to go and spoil it." Sophie lowers her voice, but it is clear that she is still angry. The woman and the boy have wandered away.

"You're mean!" says Trudie. Her eyes fill with tears.

"Oh, now she's going to cry," says Sophie. "Crybaby!"

"I . . . am . . . not . . . a crybaby!" Trudie says. But she starts to cry anyway, big, fat tears that streak her face and drip off her chin.

I am stunned. I have never seen Sophie so upset with Trudie. It's a little frightening.

"That's enough, Sophie," says Mama sharply. "I think we have to leave. Now."

"What about our presents?" Sophie asks. "You promised."

"Yes, I did. But not if you girls are going to fight this way."

I look at Trudie, who is trying so hard to stop her tears. Suddenly, I am struck by just how young she really is. Why, she was even afraid of the ticket chopper. Trudie doesn't *mean* to be so much trouble, I realize with some surprise. She just can't help it. I feel a strange, new tenderness toward my baby sister.

"May I say something?" I ask Mama.

"All right," Mama agrees.

"Sophie, you really want the tea set, don't you?" I say to my big sister. She nods.

I get another surprise when I see that there are tears in *her* eyes, too.

"But, Trudie, you're not sure if you want it. And it's hard for you to figure out if you want it when Sophie is so angry at you."

"That's right," says Trudie. "It *is* nice. . . . But I'm still not sure. . . ."

"Do you remember the tea party we had the day that it rained?"

"We had fun," Trudie says. Her voice is still quivery, but her tears have stopped.

"We did! And if we had this tea set, a real tea set, we could have fun like that again. Maybe even more fun," I say. She is quiet, so I go on. "Look. Can I just show it to you one more time?" Together we look at the set. "I think Angelica Grace would really like these dishes. And the napkins, too."

"She would . . ." Trudie wipes her eyes with the back of her hand. Carefully, she lifts up two small spoons. "We can let the dolls stir their tea with these. Or if we make a cake they can cut it with the knives and forks."

"Are you saying yes, then?" Sophie asks. But she asks in a gentle voice.

"I am," Trudie says cautiously.

"Trudie, are you very sure this is what you want?" Papa asks.

"Very sure." This time, she does sound sure.

Mama looks at the price tag again and shows it to Papa. He looks at us and then at Mama and nods. Then he brings the tea set to the cash register. We all follow along. Mama gives my shoulders a squeeze. Sophie's mouth is, I notice, slightly open, as if she is still surprised at how things have worked out. Trudie slips her hand into mine as we walk. It feels small and warm.

"Thank you," she whispers.

"You're welcome," I whisper back.

⚬⚬⚬⚬⚬⚬

Our picnic in the park is so much fun. Papa sings funny little songs for us. Mama points out the birds she recognizes—a robin with his red breast, a blue jay with his bright feathers. After we have eaten the sandwiches and the pickles, Trudie pokes around in our picnic basket.

"What are you looking for?" Papa asks her.

"Dessert," she says, continuing to hunt.

"Dessert? Why, I didn't know you girls liked dessert,"

Papa says. But you can tell he's teasing her.

"Where did you hide it, Papa?" says Trudie. She's abandoned the basket and is pulling on Papa's hand.

"Over there," Papa says. He points toward a bald, tubby man selling ice cream cones from a cart.

"Ice cream!" cries Trudie, and she runs ahead while Sophie and I help Mama gather up our things.

When we all reach the cart, Sophie picks chocolate and Trudie picks strawberry. I am torn between vanilla, my favorite flavor, and strawberry, because Trudie's looks so tempting. After standing there for five minutes while everyone waits for me to choose, I finally decide to get vanilla. I know it will taste good. I tell myself that I can get strawberry another time, even though ice cream is a special treat and we don't have it very often. I am just about to take a lick when Trudie yanks on my sleeve.

"Here," she says, holding her cone up toward my face. "You can try some of mine."

"Delicious," I say, swirling my tongue across the creamy, cold pink of it. "Just delicious."

# 4

## BAD NEWS

The last day of school comes in June. All of our lessons are finished. There is a special assembly in the auditorium, and then each of the classes has a party to celebrate. Sophie, Trudie, and I have on our best lightweight dresses, the ones we wear to *shul* in the summer. Mine is red with dark blue stripes; Trudie's is made of the same material, but somehow, with her golden brown curls, the colors look better on her. Sophie's dress is made of ivory cotton with tiny blue forget-me-nots embroidered on it; Mama used leftover fabric from one of her own dresses. I wish I had a dress like that, but there wasn't enough fabric for me.

Once I am in my classroom, I don't think about the dress anymore. My teacher has brought in cupcakes from a bakery on Grand Street; they are frosted with buttercream and sprinkled with sugar. Batya gives me a belated birthday present—an embroidered handkerchief—and Esther invites me to come over to her apartment next week. Sophie, Trudie, and I stroll home together, talking about our class parties. The air is warm and soft; the sky is blue with only a handful of puffy clouds. Summer feels like it is really here.

Now that school is over, we settle into our new routine. In the mornings, we all do chores in the doll shop. The shop stays busy with customers. Some are from our own neighborhood, but others come all the way from the Bronx or Queens or even New Jersey. Goldie greets each new arrival with a series of merry chirps.

In the afternoons, when our chores are done, we can play. We go out on the street, where sometimes someone has pried the cover off a fire hydrant and the water gushes up and out into the gutter. We take turns running through the icy spray, and then run home to towel off and change out of our wet dresses.

On the Fourth of July, along with Mama and Papa, we climb up onto the roof to watch the fireworks. Although it is usually forbidden, Papa allows us to bring our special dolls and the tea set up with us. We give the dolls root beer in the cups and broken pretzel sticks on the plates; of course, we do the drinking and eating for them. We tap the cups together in a toast, just like we have seen grown-ups do, and we rub our fingers over the plates to get up every last bit of salt. Above us, the night sky blooms with glittering streaks of red, blue, and gold.

By the end of July, we are all tired of the heat. One Sunday we take the streetcar to Coney Island, where we splash in the waves and eat cotton candy on the board-walk. But most days, we are content to play quietly with the dolls. Sometimes we pretend they are dancers or sing-ers on the stage; other times, they are princesses in a royal court. We use the tea set in almost all our games; Trudie always says how glad she is that we bought it. One day, she accidentally drops a plate and it breaks in two. Her face pales with fear as we both wait for Sophie to explode. But Sophie only says, "If Papa can fix china dolls, I'll bet he can fix china plates, too."

Trudie is so relieved that she jumps up and hugs Sophie, who looks surprised, but hugs her back.

During the school year, Papa always gets up early and goes to the newsstand on the corner to get his newspaper. In the summer, though, it is my job to get the paper for him. I don't mind at all; getting the paper is kind of fun. Solly, the man at the newsstand, usually rolls the paper into a cone and hands it to me with a bow, like it's a bunch of flowers. Sometimes he even gives me a piece of penny candy—a peppermint ball or a lemon drop—and I get to eat it on the way home.

But on the morning of August second, I go to the newsstand and Solly doesn't even seem to know who I am. He just hands me the paper in an absentminded sort of way, and if I didn't tell him twice, he would have forgotten to take my money. I look longingly at the rock candy, the gumdrops, and licorice but Solly doesn't pay any attention. I check my pocket—sometimes I have a penny tucked inside—but no such luck. I sigh and walk home slowly in the heat, paper tucked under my arm. Then I see it: a penny on the sidewalk, winking up at me. A penny! Now I can run back to Solly's and buy candy after all. As I kneel down to get the penny, I drop the paper, which flops open. The headline is in huge letters:

GERMANY DECLARES WAR ON RUSSIA
FEAR THAT FRANCE IS NEXT

I have never seen such big letters on a newspaper before. This must be important. Very important. I forget about going back to Solly's for candy and instead run the rest of the way home and take the stairs two at a time. By the time I reach our door, I am out of breath and panting a little. Everyone is at the breakfast table. Sophie is dipping her bread into her tea, and Trudie is taking advantage of Mama's turned back to stick her spoon into the jam jar. I hand Papa the newspaper. I see his eyes get wide and his mouth shrink to a tight, worried line. Silently Papa hands it to Mama. She looks at the headline and then pushes the paper away. "So it's finally come," Papa says quietly. Mama doesn't reply.

"What's come? What's happened?" says Trudie. There is a dot of jam on her chin.

"The war," Papa answers.

"What war, Papa?" asks Sophie.

"In Europe," he explains. "Germany and Russia are fighting."

"Will it come here?" I ask. I sit down at my place, next to Sophie. To my surprise, she grabs my hand and squeezes it tightly before letting go. Mama has placed a slice of jam-covered bread on my plate, but I suddenly seem to have lost my appetite.

"I don't think so," Papa says. "But the Germans will invade France, too—that much is clear. And we have family in Russia: Mama's brothers and sister, my two brothers. You girls have a lot of cousins you've never even met."

"I don't want them to get hurt, Mama," Trudie says.

"We don't want anyone to get hurt," Mama says, more to herself than to Trudie.

Trudie looks at Mama, and her bottom lip quivers.

But before she can actually begin crying, I reach over and touch her on the shoulder. "Don't be scared," I tell her, trying to sound calm. It isn't easy; I am scared, too. "Everything will be all right." Will it? I don't really know, but it is the only thing I can think of to say. Trudie's lip stops quivering as she gets up from the table, walks over to me, and plops down in my lap. I let out a loud, showy sigh. But secretly, I am glad. Ever since that day at F.A.O. Schwartz, things have been different with Trudie and me. It's as if now she looks up to me, too, not just Sophie. "Just don't get any jam on me," I tell her. She nods and then uses my napkin to wipe her face.

Despite the news about the war, everything seems to be normal for the next few weeks. Summer vacation will be over soon. Sophie, Trudie, and I spend our time helping Mama, playing in the doll shop, or trying to stay cool in the stifling heat. Sophie and I take turns putting each other's hair up, and we both comb and style Trudie's hair—anything to get it off our necks. But one night, after dinner, Papa asks us to join him in the parlor. He looks so serious that my heart starts to thump a little faster as we follow him in.

"You all know about the war," Papa begins.

"We do, Papa," says Sophie.

"Well, even though America is not fighting, the war will still affect us here."

"How, Papa?" I ask.

"Doll parts," he says. "The parts we use come from Germany. And because of the war, we won't be able to get them. Not for a long time, anyway."

"Why not?" asks Trudie.

"Because America is going to stop trading with Germany. That's what happens when countries go to war. Everything suffers."

There is a long, heavy silence while we try to make sense of what he has just said.

"How can you fix the dolls without the parts, Papa?" Trudie finally asks.

"I can't," says Papa. "At least, I can't repair any dolls whose parts I don't have here already."

"How many dolls is that?" Sophie asks. I glance over at her worried face.

"I'm not sure," he says. "I'll have to check."

"If you and Mama can't fix dolls, what will happen to the shop? And what will happen to us?" asks Sophie. Those are the exact questions I want to ask, but I am afraid to hear the answers.

"I'm not sure," Papa says again, looking down at his hands as if he doesn't quite know what to do with them anymore.

<hr>

It turns out that there are twenty-three dolls in the shop. For the next week, Papa and Mama work extra hard to fix all the ones whose parts are there—that totals ten. When they are done, the mended dolls are picked up or sent back to their homes. Thirteen dolls are left stranded.

Papa takes out a box of file cards. The cards have the names and addresses of the dolls' owners printed in black ink. Papa and Mama write notes to each of the owners, asking what to do with the dolls. Some of the owners come into the shop and take their broken dolls home. I think the dolls seem sad to be leaving before they have been made whole again. Some owners who live in far-off places like New Jersey or Connecticut ask that Papa mail back their dolls, which he does, packing them carefully in double boxes and lots of straw. In the end, there are six dolls left in the shop: Angelica Grace, Victoria Marie, and Bernadette Louise are among them.

"How odd that they all stayed," says Sophie. Papa has just left for the post office with the last of the dolls to be mailed, Mama is upstairs, and we girls are in the doll shop. With so many of the dolls gone, the shop looks empty and unfamiliar.

"It's like they were meant for us," I say.

"Wouldn't it be wonderful if it were true?" asks Sophie.

"If only we could keep them . . ." says Trudie,

looking deep into Angelica Grace's face. I touch my finger to the crack in Bernadette Marie's glazed white arm but say nothing more.

We stop going down to the doll shop to play. Instead, we try extra hard to help Mama. She has started taking in sewing for some of our neighbors, like Mrs. Kornblatt and Mrs. Mirsky, who live upstairs, and Mrs. Rogoff, who is my friend Esther's mother. Soon our apartment is filled with baskets of clothes to be mended or altered. I overhear Papa and Mama arguing in Yiddish. I hear one word—*gelt*—over and over again, so I ask Sophie what it means. She tells me it means *money*.

One night, I am unable to fall asleep. Even though it's late and I'm tired, I just can't settle down. The bedroom is hot and stuffy, and Trudie snores. I hear rustling in the dark and say, "Are you up?" to Sophie.

"I'm up," she says.

There is more rustling and then Trudie says sleepily, "Me too." In a minute, though, she is snoring again.

"I'm worried about Papa and Mama," I confess.

"So am I," Sophie says.

"But what can we do?"

Then I hear a click and someone opens the door. Mama.

"Girls, aren't you supposed to be sleeping? Why do I hear voices?"

"Sorry, Mama," says Sophie. "It's just too hot to sleep."

"Would you like to sleep on the roof tonight, then?" asks Mama. Instead of answering, Sophie and I start bouncing up and down on our beds.

The noise wakes Trudie, who looks up and says, "Why are you bothering me?" But Sophie and I are already gathering pillows and blankets and following Mama out the window and up the fire escape. Trudie drags herself out of bed and stumbles behind. This is not the first time we have slept on the roof, but it's always a big treat when we do. It's much cooler up there, and we love the view of the streets below. Sometimes, other families join us, but tonight, we have it all to ourselves.

Mama goes back down to get the big, soft feather beds she had when she was a girl in Russia. We love to hear stories about her little village in "the old country." Mama used to tend geese, and the feathers in our beds come

from the fat, noisy birds that lived half a world away.

When we are all settled into the cozy beds she makes for us, she plants a kiss on each of our foreheads and says, "Now go to sleep! Papa and I will be up soon."

Trudie falls back to sleep right away, but Sophie and I wait until Mama has been gone for a few minutes and then start talking again.

"Maybe we could get jobs," I say.

"What kind of jobs?"

"We could help out some of the ladies Mama sews for. Wash the dishes or run errands. Mrs. Kornblatt has a baby. We could watch her sometimes." I have seen the baby with her white bonnet, white booties, and plump, pink cheeks. It would be fun to look after her for a little while.

"Anna, that is not going to help," Sophie says in that I'm-so-much-smarter-than-you tone that always stings. "We need to make some real money, not pocket change."

"It was just an idea," I say, feeling snubbed.

"Well, it's not a very good one, so keep thinking."

I don't say anything but just look up at the sky. I can see the stars and the pale, white dime of the moon. At first, Sophie was so grateful that I was able to persuade Trudie to agree to the tea set, she was really nice to me. But it seems that's over now. After a while I realize that Sophie is asleep. I am the only one awake until Mama and Papa climb the fire escape to join us. Papa. How to help Papa. How? The question keeps circling around and around in my mind until my eyelids start to feel heavy, and I drift off into dreamland.

# 5

## PITCHING IN

The next morning, I am the last one to sit down to breakfast. Mama has already poured Papa's coffee and filled our glasses with milk. "Come and eat," Mama urges, passing the plate piled high with freshly baked bread. She was up late last night, kneading the dough and letting it rise. The smell fills the room.

"Thank you, Mama," I say. I start to butter a slice, but I am so eager to talk to Papa that I end up getting butter all over my fingers and have to lick it off.

"Papa," I say excitedly. "Papa, I know *exactly* what we can do in a doll repair shop without dolls or doll parts."

"And what would that be?" he asks with a small smile. I can see that he doesn't believe I could have thought of something that could actually work.

"We should make some dolls! But not dolls out of bisque or china or anything else that comes from Germany. And then we could sell them."

Papa is all set to chuckle, but I guess something about my expression stops him. "Make dolls?" he asks.

"Yes, Papa! Make them!"

"Out of what?"

"Cloth, stuffing, felt. Things we have or could get."

"Well, it's very sweet of you to want to help, but I don't think—"

"That's a very good idea!" Mama says before Papa can finish. "I was actually thinking about it myself. After all, I can sew. And I did make those rag dolls for you girls, remember? We could start with something simple. It would be better than sitting here and worrying about what we're going to do next."

"We could all pitch in, Mama!" says Sophie. "I know we could!" She looks at me as if to say, *I'm impressed*.

"I'll help," I say.

"Me too!" Trudie chimes in.

"Well, maybe we *could* come up with a simple pattern

for a doll. Dress her in clothes Mama makes. The hair could be yarn. . . ." Papa says, as though he is thinking out loud.

We talk about the dolls we want to make all through breakfast, and when we are finished eating and washing up, we march down to the doll shop while Papa prepares a shopping list that reads:

2 rolls buckram
1 roll muslin
2 sheets felt—different colors
1 skein brown wool

I know that muslin is a kind of cotton, but I've never seen the word *buckram* before, so I ask Papa what it means. He explains that it's coarse linen, useful for bookbinding, and, in our case, dolls. Trudie thinks it a funny word, and she repeats it a few times. Pretty soon it sounds like nonsense, and we are all giggling as we say it with her: *buckram, buckram.*

Papa leaves to go shopping, and we girls sit down at his workbench. Goldie tweets and twitters madly when we get near him; he's been lonely. Mama gives each of us a large sheet of paper. From a drawer behind the counter, she pulls out her long, flat tin of colored pencils.

"Are we making paper dolls, Mama?" asks Trudie.

"In a way," she says. "First, we have to have an idea of what our dolls are going to look like. So you are all going to draw your ideas for dolls on the paper. Then we'll pick out the ones we like best and see if we can sew them."

"I don't know what to draw," says Trudie. Uh-oh—that whiny sound again. But then I remember that Trudie looks up to me now. I can help her.

"Anything you like," I explain. "It can be a character from a book or a song or a play. Or something you make up, like a mermaid or a fairy."

"Oh, I see . . ." Trudie says, and I receive a grateful smile from Mama. We all take pencils and begin to sketch. When Papa returns, we are eager to show him our drawings.

"Look at mine first!" crows Trudie, waving the paper in front of Papa's face.

"Let me put my packages down," Papa says. He sets his bag on the floor; I can see the muslin and the brown wool sticking out from the top. He takes Trudie's drawing and studies it.

"I see . . . a queen," he says, studying the drawing.

"Actually, she's a fairy, Papa. See her wings?" Trudie says.

I'm pleased; I guess she liked my idea well enough to use it.

"A fairy. Of course," Papa says, and Trudie smiles.

"*Mine* is a queen," says Sophie.

"Yes," says Papa. "What a fine crown and ermine-trimmed cloak she has." Then he turns to me. "What did you draw, Anna?"

"A nurse," I say, handing him my drawing.

"A nurse?" Papa asks.

"Yes, Papa, you know. A nurse like the brave nurses who care for the wounded soldiers."

"Oh yes, I see," says Papa, looking at Mama thoughtfully. "A nurse. That's very original. And timely."

By this time, it is already past noon and we are all hungry, so we go upstairs for lunch, which is borscht—cold beet soup—and bread. After we have eaten, Mama and Papa want to look at the drawings again, so Mama lays them all out on the table. There they are—the fairy, the queen, and my nurse, with her white pointed cap and navy-blue cape.

"I think we should make the nurse doll," says Sophie. I am stunned. I thought she would want to do the queen, because it was her idea.

"Why?" asks Papa.

"Because she's so original. You said so yourself, Papa. No one else will think of making a nurse doll."

"Let's make the nurse!" Trudie chimes in.

"So you like her, too?" Papa asks.

"I do. Anna has good ideas," Trudie says, and comes to stand next to me. I don't say anything, but inside, I am brimming with pride.

"Well, I think it's an excellent place to begin," Mama says firmly.

"So we have a plan. . . ." Papa says thoughtfully. "See if we can make a nurse doll that doesn't use any parts we can't get." He looks at all of us. "What do you say, girls? Do you think we can do it?"

I look at my sisters and we all nod.

"Yes," I reply. "I know we can."

# 6

## DOLL FACTORY

For the next few days, the doll shop is busy, busy, busy. It turns out that Papa knows a lot about making dolls' heads. All his years of fixing dolls have given him a good idea of how to do it. He started out back in Russia, in his uncle's shop, where he repaired plates, vases, and platters made of bisque, porcelain, and china. Occasionally someone would bring in a bisque or china doll with a cracked head. Papa would try to fix that, too. He became interested in how the bisque dolls were made by pouring raw materials like clay and water into molds and then firing the molds in a hot oven. When he started his own shop, he decided to mend just dolls. And now, all his experience has helped him figure out how to make a doll, even one that isn't bisque.

Papa begins to experiment. He sculpts faces from a clay he mixes from flour, water, and a little olive oil. Then he wets a sheet of buckram and drapes it over the clay form, leaving an opening at the back so he can slip the molded buckram off when it has dried.

"But the dolly will have a space at the back of her head," says Trudie, clearly bothered by the idea.

"We'll cover it with hair," Papa says.

The first doll Papa makes doesn't turn out too well— her face has a strange, flattened look.

"Like someone punched her in the nose," says Trudie, and she's right. So Papa tries again. And again. The fourth time, he finally makes one we all like: even without her painted features, we can see that she has full, round cheeks, a pert chin, and a nicely curved forehead.

Mama works on the pattern for the bodies, and we help with the sewing. We all know how to sew, even Trudie, though her thimble is too big and she has to wrap her finger with a bit of cloth to keep it from slipping off. We try different kinds of stuffing: tissue paper and straw by themselves are too crinkly, sawdust is too stiff. Finally we settle on a mix of all three: tissue paper at the center, then some straw, and finally the sawdust. After the stuffing process is done, there is more cutting as well as more sewing, pasting, and painting. Using the felt Papa bought and snippets from Mama's scrap bag, we make the nurse doll's outfit: a long, red and white striped dress; white apron; and a navy-blue cape. Best of all is the little white cap Mama makes from a piece of an old cloth napkin that she folds and starches. Trudie and I sort through Mama's button jar for the smallest buttons we can find. We use a shiny brass button for the cape and three pearly white ones for the dress.

Mama paints the face, and Papa attaches the yarn that is the doll's hair. He glues the long brown strands, and when they have dried, he twists them into a neat bun. The open space at the back of her head is now invisible. After we are all finished, we make two more nurse dolls, using the first one as our model. By the end of the day, we have three twelve-inch dolls all ready for some little girls to love. Even though Sophie is the one who usually comes up with the best names, I have the idea to call the doll Nurse Nora, and to my surprise, everyone likes the name.

"These are very fine dolls," Papa says, picking one up and admiring her. "You all did an excellent job."

Mama makes a new sign to hang in the window. It says:

NURSE NORA
HANDMADE DOLLS,
LIMITED EDITION
$1.00 EACH

But before we can start selling anything, we have to help Mama tidy up the shop, because it has turned into a real mess while we were making the dolls. As I bend down to pick up some scraps of felt from the floor, I spy a big wooden box that has been pushed aside and out of the way. I know that box. I peer inside and there are our three dolls—Victoria Marie, Bernadette Louise, and Angelica Grace—just where we left them weeks ago. It seems to me that the dolls are lonely. Bernadette Louise's mouth almost looks like it is frowning, and the black hole where Angelica Grace's eye should be seems to stare out at me.

"What are you looking at?" Sophie asks.

"Our dolls," I tell her. I reach in to take Bernadette Louise out of the box. "I was thinking that they must miss us."

"We haven't played with them in so long," Trudie says.

"Well, maybe one day they'll have company again, right, Mama?" says Sophie.

"I certainly hope so," Mama replies. When she sees the dolls, she adds, "They're all dusty." She goes upstairs and returns a few minutes later with an old worn tablecloth, stained in one corner. We clean off the dolls and put them back in the box. Mama covers them gently with the cloth.

---

The next day, the shop is back in order again. Sophie, Trudie, and I sit at Papa's workbench, waiting for people to arrive and buy our new dolls. Only they don't. The morning drags on without a single customer, and finally we trudge upstairs for lunch. In the afternoon, Sophie and Trudie don't even want to come downstairs, so I go by myself. Mama is busy with her sewing, and Papa has gone down the street to work at Mr. Bloom's grocery store. But I've been in the shop alone before; Mama is right upstairs if I need her.

I am bored, so I take one of the Nurse Nora dolls from the counter where she is displayed. Nurse Nora looks kind. And she looks like she knows how to do things, like change the dressing on a bandage or take a patient's temperature. I decide that she should meet Bernadette Louise, so I go get her from the box.

"Bernadette Louise, meet Nurse Nora," I say.

I pretend the dolls are meeting each other for the first time, shaking hands and smiling a little shyly, the way I sometimes do when I meet someone new. Pretty soon, though, they are feeling more comfortable, and I pretend they are telling each other all about how they were made and where they come from. The game is so much fun that for a minute, I don't even notice that a very stout woman in a stylish hat and a big lace collar has come into the shop and is waiting for someone—me—to assist her.

"May I help you?" I say in my most grown-up voice. I have waited on customers before and know how to use the brass cash register. But usually Papa or Mama is in the shop with me. Still, I think I can handle it all by myself.

"Yes," says the woman, who is holding a bag. "Can you fix this doll?" She pulls out a bisque lady doll with two missing arms and a badly scratched face.

"No, we can't," I say sadly. "We don't have the parts. We can't get them." I explain about the boxes that came from Germany.

"War is a terrible thing in so many ways," says the woman, shaking her head. "But thank you just the same." She puts the doll back in the bag and turns to leave. Once she is gone, the shop feels even more quiet and forlorn. Nurse Nora and Bernadette Louise look at each other, but they have nothing else to say. I put my face close to Goldie's cage; he utters a soft tweet. Then he starts chirping excitedly and hopping from perch to perch. The stout lady comes back inside; she seems to be huffing and puffing a little, maybe from the heat.

"Hello again," she says, putting down the bag and patting her brow with a hankie. "I decided that since I can't get this doll fixed, maybe I would buy a doll instead. It's for my niece; I'm seeing her later today, and she loves dolls. The sign in the window says you have dolls for sale."

"We do," I say, holding out Nurse Nora for her to see. "We have Nurse Nora dolls."

"May I see her?" The lady takes the doll in her hands and looks her over.

"She's new," I explain. "And she's part of a limited edition." That's what the sign in the window says, and I am proud that I remembered it.

"Limited edition," repeats the lady. She continues to examine Nurse Nora. "She's very sweet. And I like her clothes, too." She tilts her head and holds the doll at arm's length. "I'll take her."

"That will be one dollar, please." I wrap the doll in some tissue paper Papa keeps under the counter and hand her to her new owner. I made a sale, all by myself. I can't wait to tell Mama and Papa!

Mama and Papa are very pleased that I sold a doll, and the next morning, we girls help make another one to replace her. Then I seat myself behind the counter while Papa goes off, glumly, it seems to me, to Mr. Bloom's store. Usually Papa is so good-natured and patient. But for weeks, he has been grumpy. Just yesterday, he yelled at Trudie when she spilled her milk. Mama comforted her by explaining that Papa is just short-tempered because he's worried about the shop and what will become of it.

Certainly it is quiet without the business we used to have. Quiet and dull. The morning after I sold the first Nurse Nora, I was so excited; I was sure I was going to sell the other two dolls right away. But I didn't sell any dolls that day, the next day, or the day after that. So now I am discouraged. Mama is upstairs in the parlor, busy with her sewing. Sophie and Trudie are in our room, where Sophie is reading to Trudie. I remain in the shop with loyal little Goldie and Bernadette Louise, who are good company. I take the tea set out and invent a new make-believe game: Bernadette Louise is a servant in a very grand house with marble floors, heavy silk drapes, and crystal chandeliers. Only poor Bernadette Louise can't enjoy any of this luxury—she has to work all the time, trudging up and down a long flight of steps to bring tea and cake to her spoiled mistress. When Mama calls me upstairs for supper, I am sorry to have to leave the game behind.

The next day, I go down to the quiet shop and pick up the game where I left off. I add more details to the story of Bernadette Louise and the spoiled, mean mistress. I pretend that Bernadette Louise is really a princess in disguise, though no one knows that. She has been exiled from her throne and forced to work like a slave. She misses her family, her silky cocker spaniels, and her big bed with its frilly coverlet. And she is so hungry! The mean mistress gives Bernadette Louise only the nasty leftovers and scraps, while she stuffs her own face with cream puffs and strudel. Poor Bernadette Louise is so desperate for food that she decides she will steal one of the pastries in the kitchen, the golden éclair with chocolate glaze and the rich, delicious custard inside—

"Excuse me, but where can I find a Nurse Nora doll?" says a deep voice.

Startled, I look up to see who has spoken. It is a well-dressed man in a tan suit and shiny leather shoes. The watch peeking out of his vest pocket looks like it is made of gold.

"You want to see Nurse Nora?" I say. Quickly I tuck Bernadette Louise under the counter, out of sight. I must have been so absorbed by my game that I didn't even notice when Goldie started singing.

"Yes. A friend of my daughter's brought her Nurse Nora over to our home and I was curious, so I asked where she came from."

"Here she is," I say, and hand him the doll. I wonder why he wants to know. Most men are not interested in dolls. But this man is. He looks Nurse Nora over carefully—front and back, top of her head down to tips of her toes. Then he turns her upside down and examines her underclothes. How rude! I am about to call Mama to come down when he places her back on the counter.

"Do you have any more like this?"

"Two more," I say, showing him the other dolls we have made.

He looks those over, too, and then places them beside the first doll.

"I'll take them all," he says, reaching into the pocket of his jacket for his money. "Can you wrap them?"

"I can't sell them all," I say. We need to keep one doll so we will be able to make more. That's what Papa and Mama told me.

"No? Why not?" He's not angry; he really seems curious. So I tell him.

He thinks for a minute before he speaks again. "How about this—I'll pay for all three but won't take them all today. I'll leave you one as a model so you can make more. Then I'll come back and get it."

"I guess so," I say. "I mean, yes." I am thrilled he is buying them but also confused. Why does he need three dolls? What will he do with all of them? I am trying to figure all this out as I wrap two of the dolls in tissue. Then he hands me three crisp dollar bills and a small white card.

"I'll be back," he says, as he takes his package and walks out the door.

After he is gone, I stare at the money. Three dollar

bills. I don't think I have ever seen three dollars all to-gether before. I start to climb the stairs, eager to show Mama. Then I look at the card. It says:

Mr. Ira Greenfield
Head Buyer
F.A.O. Schwartz
Fifth Avenue and Thirty-first Street
New York City

"Mama!" I call before I am even up the stairs. "Mama, you won't believe what just happened!"

# 7

## $\mathcal{T}$HE ONES WHO STAYED

Mr. Greenfield keeps his promise and comes back two days later to pick up the third Nurse Nora doll. By the time he arrives, we have made three more dolls; they sit neatly on their shelf, ready to greet him.

"Do you have any other kinds of dolls?" Mr. Greenfield asks Papa.

"We have designs for others," says Papa. I know he is thinking of the other dolls we drew. "But we haven't actually made them yet."

"I'd be interested in seeing those when they're finished," says Mr. Greenfield as he takes the Nurse Nora dolls, wrapped and bagged, under his arm. "I'm going to try to sell these at the store, and if they do well, I want to start selling the others, too."

Our dolls, for sale at F.A.O. Schwartz! Papa looks so happy. After Mr. Greenfield leaves, he gives each of us a hug.

"We did this together," Papa says. "I couldn't have done it alone." Then he takes out the drawings of the queen and the fairy. "We need to start making these others," he says. So that is just what we do.

In September, school starts. I'm in fifth grade now, and my classroom is next door to the seventh grade, where Sophie is; Trudie's third-grade class in on the floor above us. Batya and Esther are both in my class again; we haven't seen each other in a while, and we have so much to talk about. My teacher, Miss Abbott, has springy red hair that is always escaping from its bun, and the bluest eyes. I don't even mind arithmetic so much anymore; Miss Abbott has a way of explaining things so that I really can understand.

Little by little, the doll shop becomes a doll factory. Papa gets two old tables from Mr. Karnofsky, the junk man who comes around with his gentle old horse, Bessie, and the shelves that once held broken dolls and boxes of parts now hold bolts of fabric and baskets of other materials used to make the new cloth dolls. Papa and Mama spend their time cutting, sewing, stuffing, and painting. Some of our neighbors pitch in with the work. In exchange, Mama does their sewing for free. Soon, queen dolls and fairy dolls join Nurse Nora on the shelves. Mr. Greenfield comes back and buys two more nurse dolls, as well as three queen dolls and three fairy dolls. "People are asking for them," he says.

Other customers sometimes come in and buy dolls, too. The stout lady who bought the first Nurse Nora returns with her niece and two of her niece's friends. Maybe they tell other people about our dolls, because soon more girls are coming in and asking for them. Goldie sings and chirps all day; he likes the activity. Sophie, Trudie, and I help out, too. There is hardly any time to spend playing with our dolls in the shop anymore, no more make-believe or let's-pretend. The yellow tea set is packed away in its woven straw basket. I put Bernadette Louise back in her box with the other dolls. Even though I am not playing with her, I like knowing she's there, waiting for me. Sometimes I write her little notes saying *Miss you* or *We'll have a tea party again soon*, and tuck them into the box with the dolls. Writing to someone, even a doll, brings you closer to them.

"Papa, do you think the war will ever end?" asks Trudie one day as she is helping bundle small bits of yarn for hair.

"Mama and I pray for that day all the time," he answers. I know that he received a letter from his brother recently, and he is so grateful that for now, everyone back in "the old country" is all right. "Why do you ask?"

"I just wondered whether you would ever start fixing dolls again. Whether the shop would ever be like it used to."

"I hope it will," he says. "In the meantime, we're lucky that we can do something else instead."

I read the papers now—not just the headlines—after Papa has finished. I skip over the hard words, trying to understand what is going on. And though I would not say it out loud, I don't think the fighting is going to end any time soon. Germany marched into Belgium; Japan declared war on Germany. The poor soldiers dig trenches and climb inside to shoot at the enemy. I can't think about it too much because it makes me frightened and sad.

Fall is filled with Jewish holidays. A few weeks after school begins, it is Rosh Hashanah, the Jewish New Year. The evening of the holiday, Mama roasts a chicken, and for dessert we dip apples in honey, to sweeten the coming year. They are so sticky and good. In the morning, we go to *shul*. Ten days later, it is Yom Kippur, the day of atonement. Rosh Hashanah is a happy holiday but Yom Kippur is serious; we spend the day in *shul* and the grown-ups fast. Even the children's service with Miss Epstein is more restrained. Although no one tells me to do this, I silently ask God if he will please, please do something about the war. I feel better afterward, even though nothing happens right away. Mama always says that God works in mysterious ways. I hope that she is right.

As soon as Yom Kippur is over, we start to get ready for Sukkos, the seven-day festival of the harvest. Papa builds a *sukkah*—a three-sided stall with a thatched roof—outside on the tiny patch of tightly packed dirt in back of the doll shop. Mama has tried many times to plant a garden in the spot, but the soil is bad and there is very little light because of all the buildings around us. Still, there is enough room for the wooden poles of the *sukkah*, and after Papa puts the leaves of the roof on, we all help to decorate it with the fruits and vegetables Mama buys from the neighborhood pushcarts.

One day during Sukkos, we decide to bring our dolls out back. We know we are not supposed to do this, but I have invented a game that we all want badly to play. We pretend the dolls are magical elves that live in an enchanted forest; they have the power to make the apples and pears on the roof of the *sukkah* grow huge, and they use the giant fruit to feed everyone who is hungry—

Papa comes through the back door. "Why are these dolls outside?" he asks.

Oh no—we've been caught.

"I'm sorry, Papa," I say. "It was my idea. I know we shouldn't have done it."

Papa looks at me sternly, and then at the dolls. They do look like they are having a good time.

"Well," he says, a little less sternly now, "don't let it happen again." Then he asks, "Are these the unclaimed dolls?"

"Three of them, Papa. There are three more."

"Oh, yes. I remember now. I'll have to write to their owners again."

We abandon the game and follow Papa inside. He goes to his oak card file, copies out the addresses onto the cream-colored envelopes, and writes six letters. Three of those letters go to the owners of Angelica Grace, Victoria Marie, and Bernadette Louise.

"What will happen if they don't answer this time?" asks Sophie.

"Let's wait and see," says Papa. But I have already begun to hope that somehow, some way, Bernadette Louise will actually become mine.

A week later, Papa receives the first reply. It seems that Angelica Grace's owners do not want the broken doll back. They have bought their daughter a new doll, and they tell Papa that he may keep this one if he likes. The following day, the letter that was sent to Victoria Marie's owner comes back unopened, with a large black stamp that reads: RETURN TO SENDER. ADDRESS UN-KNOWN. Replies to the letters about Bernadette Louise and the other unclaimed dolls never come at all.

"Well," says Papa, "I guess that means the dolls belong to you girls. They haven't been claimed, and I think it's fair enough that you keep them."

We are seated at the table, having an after-school snack of rice pudding. At Papa's words, Trudie jumps up and pushes her bowl away.

"Really, Papa? Really and truly?" She is hopping from one foot to the other.

"Really," says Papa. Trudie and Sophie look at each another. Then they clatter down the stairs, eager to see their dolls. Only I remain where I am, looking up at Papa.

"What about Bernadette Louise?" I ask. I know Papa said "you girls," but after all, there was never any reply about my doll; maybe he will tell me I have to wait until there is.

"You know, that doll has been here for nearly a year. I wrote to her owner twice and never did hear back. I think that's long enough to wait, don't you?"

"You mean . . . ?"

"Yes, she is yours," he answers. I hug him tightly before I run downstairs. Papa seems more like Papa these days: warm, patient, and kind. He didn't even get too angry when we broke the rule about taking the dolls out of the shop.

"Thank you, Papa!" I call over my shoulder. "Thank you so much!" A store-bought china doll of my very own—I can hardly believe it's for real.

# 8

## GONE

Now that we actually own our dolls, we want to fix them, not let them stay broken. But Mama and Papa are too busy making new dolls to help us, so one day after school, Sophie, Trudie, and I decide to try on our own. Even though Papa said there were no more parts, we will look one more time. We hunt inside cabinets and behind the counter, on shelves and in the closet, searching for any parts that Papa might have missed. After twenty minutes, we are ready to give up when Sophie spots a box way up on the top shelf; it is nearly hidden by a basket of yarn that sits in front of it. The only reason she can see it at all is because she has climbed up on a chair to look. But the chair is wobbly, and she gets down. I find the stepladder and hold it steady for her.

"Careful!" Trudie says, and I have to smile because she sounds so much like Mama. Sophie *is* careful and brings the box down slowly. It is covered with dust, and we all start to sneeze. But it is worth it: inside are treasures.

"Look!" says Sophie, as she holds up a small package wrapped in cotton wool. Eagerly, we unwrap it. Dolls' eyes. Angelica Grace needs an eye. But two of these are brown, and the wrong size anyway. The other is blue and looks as if it will fit, but it is not the same shade of blue as Angelica Grace's existing eye.

"What else is in here?" I ask. We find a wig, a few dusty arms, and several legs.

"Not exactly what we need . . ." says Trudie. But to my astonishment, there is not a trace of a whine in her voice. Instead, she adds, "Maybe we can use them anyway."

"Maybe we can," says Sophie. "We can show Papa and see what he thinks."

"I had no idea these were here!" Papa exclaims when we bring the parts upstairs. "If I had known, I might have been able to fix some of the dolls I sent back. But as long as you've found them, we might as well use them now."

"When can we do it, Papa?" asks Trudie. "Today? Right now?"

Papa smiles. "Give me a little time," he says. "And remember—these parts aren't the right ones; the results won't be perfect."

"They'll be perfect for us," I tell him, and my sisters nod eagerly in agreement.

Papa carves out a bit of time each day to work on our dolls. He inserts the eye—a deep, dark blue—into Angelica's hollow socket. Even though the colors don't match, she looks interesting and even mysterious. He is able to use the wig—it's a pretty shade of strawberry blonde, not unlike her original color—for Victoria Marie. The wig is too large, but Mama fixes that by taking it in with a needle and thread. And to replace Victoria Marie's missing clothes, Mama uses scraps from her basket to sew new ones—a long black-and-white polka dot dress, a white apron, and undergarments, too. Papa can't replace the doll's legs—he doesn't have ones that are the right size—but he files down the broken toes, and Mama paints them to match the color of Victoria Marie's skin. Then Sophie figures out how to sew her some shoes using bits of black felt and snipped-down pieces of her own worn-out shoelaces. Finally, Papa shows her how to use a bit of wire to attach shiny black beads to the two holes in the doll's ears.

My doll, Bernadette Louise, is given a new left foot to replace the missing one, though the two feet look quite different. And although Papa can't fix her cracked arm, I add some lace trim to the sleeve of her dress—which I have washed, sewn, and ironed—and that completely hides the crack. By Thursday, all three dolls have been mended.

"There!" I say proudly. "They look just grand!"

"They do," agrees Sophie.

"But what about the other three dolls?" Trudie asks.

"There are *other* dolls?" asks Mama.

We bring the other three dolls so that Mama can see. Two are baby dolls—I don't know why, but I've never liked baby dolls—and the other is a tiny boy doll, the kind you would use in a dollhouse. Still, they need fixing, so it seems only right that we should fix them. One of the babies has a cracked head, and both are very dirty. It's easy enough to wash them off, and Mama disguises the crack with an old baby bonnet that belonged to Trudie. The other baby doll is missing both legs. Papa doesn't have any more doll legs that fit, but suddenly, I have an idea: using an old square napkin, I wrap the doll up as if she were a real baby wrapped in a blanket. Everyone agrees this is a very good solution. The tiny boy doll is also missing a leg, but because he wears long pants, it's easier to stuff some old cloth into the pants leg to fill it out. He is still without a foot, but Papa fixes that by carving and shaping a small piece of cork and then painting it black, to match the doll's other shoe.

"That's better," Trudie says, when all those dolls are fixed, too. "But what do we do with them?"

Mama and Papa look at each other. It seems like they haven't thought of that.

"We could keep them here and try to sell them," Sophie says.

"It might be hard to sell them in this condition," says Papa.

"Mr. Karnofosky might buy them, though," I say.

Mr. Karnofksy buys and sells old stuff that people are getting rid of. We got our worktables from him.

"Now that's a good plan," Papa says. "I'm sure he'll give us something for them. Not a lot, but something." Papa looks at his watch. "He should be by very soon, too."

When Mr. Karnofsky comes down the street with Bessie and his wagon, tooting his long tin horn, Papa steps outside to flag him down. Mr. Karnofsky stops in front of our building.

"Hey, Breittlemann," he says to Papa, clapping him on the back. "What have you got for me today?"

"Anna, can you show Mr. Karnofsky what we have?"

I give him the dolls, one at a time. He looks them over very carefully and then reaches into his pocket and pulls out a quarter.

"How's that?" he asks, handing the money to Papa but looking at me.

"That's just fine," says Papa. They seal the deal with a handshake, and Papa gives Sophie, Trudie, and me a penny a piece for candy.

"A penny! I want to spend it right now!" Trudie says.

"Is that all right, Mama?" Sophie asks. "Can we get some candy now?"

"What if we went to the bakery instead?" I say, before Mama can even answer. "We could buy some fancy cookies and have a doll tea party. We haven't had one in such a long time."

"A party!" says Trudie, "That's even better than plain old candy. Can we, Mama? Please? Can we?"

"I guess that would be all right," Mama says.

Papa and Mama have finished working for the day, so Trudie and I go back inside and clean off one of the tables, while Sophie goes around the corner to Zeitlin's Bakery on Grand Street to get the cookies. Then Mama and Trudie go upstairs. Mama has some mending to do before supper, and Trudie is going to get the tea set. I am left alone in the shop, and just as I have finished wiping the counter clean someone walks in. It is an old lady wearing a dark green dress and long, dark gloves. Her hat is dark, too, and adorned with a few faded but soft looking flowers. She moves slowly, one hand resting on a silver-tipped cane.

"Hello, may I help you?" I say. I remember Mr. Greenfield's visit; I'm good with customers.

"Is this Breittlemann's Doll Repair Shop?" the woman asks.

"Yes, but we aren't taking any dolls to fix right now. We do have some new dolls to sell, though." I pick up one of the fairies to show her. "See?"

"She's charming, but I'm not here to buy a doll. Or to drop one off," she says. "I'm here to pick up a doll I left some time ago. I had a note from the owner—would that be your father?" I nod, and a very slow, fluttery feeling starts in my stomach. It is not a good flutter, though. "He asked me to pick up my doll. I'm afraid I haven't been well lately, and so I didn't answer his letters. But here I am and I can take her with me today."

Now, in addition to the fluttery feeling, there is a bad feeling in my chest, like my heart is knocking against my ribs, trying to get out. And my face feels hot, the way it does when I get a fever.

"What kind of a doll is she?" I ask.

"She's a very pretty china thing. Dark hair all wound

up around her head. One of her feet is missing though, and her arm is cracked. I have the ticket right here." She holds out a creased slip of paper. But I don't need the slip of paper to know that the doll she means is Bernadette Louise.

"I'll get her." I am trembling as I go to get the doll from her box. "Here she is," I say, handing her to the woman. I am trying not to cry.

"Yes, that's her," says the woman. "But she's been mended." The woman looks confused. "In his letter, your father said that he couldn't repair her without the parts he needed."

"Well, when he didn't hear from you, he thought that . . . I mean . . . you see—"

"We thought that the doll wasn't going to be claimed, and so we let our Anna keep her." I turn to see Mama standing there by the stairs. Trudie is right behind her. Mama explains how the others were left behind, and we had just assumed this one was, too.

The woman looks down at the doll and then at us. "Did you wash and press the clothes yourself?" she asks me.

"Yes."

"And you sewed the lace on her sleeve?" the woman continues.

This time I just nod, because I am afraid if I say anything, tears will pour out, and I do *not* want to be a crybaby.

"I see her broken foot has been replaced, too."

"The girls found some leftover parts," explains Mama.

"I didn't mind that her feet don't match. I thought that Bernadette Louise would rather have the foot than not," I manage to say.

"Bernadette Louise?" asks the woman, clearly puzzled.

"The doll," I say. "That's what I called her."

"I see," says the woman. "I see." She looks down at the doll and then at me again. "Thank you for taking such good care of her."

"Would you like me to wrap her?" Mama steps over to the counter and begins looking for the paper and bags. When the woman reaches for her purse, Mama shakes her head.

"This is a kind of makeshift repair," she says. "We don't expect you to pay for it."

"But you put so much work into her," the woman protests. "I insist." She hands Mama three quarters, and Mama thanks her. Then, taking the wrapped doll, she leaves.

After she goes, I feel Mama's hand on my shoulder. I am going to cry now, I can tell, and there is nothing I can do to stop it. I suddenly understand how Trudie must feel. Although she has been crying a lot less lately, I am reminded of how hard it is to control yourself when you really need to cry.

"I'm sorry, Anna," says Mama in a gentle voice. "I know how much you loved that doll."

"Uh-huh," is all I say. The tears are hot on my face, but I don't wipe them away.

"What's wrong?" asks Sophie, who has just come back with a white bakery box of cookies.

I let Mama tell her the story. I don't feel like telling it myself.

"I'll let you play with my doll," says Sophie when Mama is done. "We can share."

"Me too," says Trudie. "We can have the tea party and you can hold Angelica Grace." This only makes me cry more. I don't want to share, and I don't want to have a tea party. Mama gives my shoulders squeeze.

"We'll find a way to get you another doll," says Mama. "You wait and see." She turns to Trudie and adds softly, "Let's have the tea party another day."

"Too bad we sold those dolls to Mr. Karnofsky," Sophie says. "Maybe we could return the money and get one of those baby dolls back."

But I don't want another doll, especially not one of those stupid old baby dolls. I want Bernadette Louise and only Bernadette Louise.

# 9

## THE LETTER

In the weeks after Bernadette Louise is taken away, I can't stop thinking about her. Mama has to ask me the same thing three times in row before I hear her. It's just as bad at school. Miss Abbott, who is always so nice, asks me to stay after class and wants to know why I have not been paying attention. Another, stricter teacher might have smacked my knuckles with a ruler, so I mumble something about having a lot to think about now. Then I tell her that I am sorry, and that I will try to do better. I can't even look at her as I say this. Instead, I have to look down at my shoes, which I was supposed to polish but didn't. They have scuff marks all over the toes, and Mama will be cross with me when she sees them.

At home, Trudie and Sophie try not to make too big a fuss about their dolls when I am around, and they are pretty good about sharing them with me. But it's not the same. I don't even want to play with their dolls. I don't really want to play with anything, it seems. Instead, I take out the twenty cents I keep hidden away in a special pouch. The money comes from different places—some of it I found, some I earned, some Papa gave me. I have not wanted to spend it on candy. I've been saving it for something really special. Now I know just what that something is. I walk to the stationer's store on Grand Street where I buy a small, ruled notebook, and I begin writing in it. This makes me feel better, so I keep doing it. I write about Bernadette Louise, school, my family, the woman who came and took my doll away. I write until my pencil point gets dull, and my hand hurts. Then I tuck the little book into the pocket of my dress, where I know it will be safe. Sometimes Sophie or Trudie asks me what I'm writing, but I don't want to say too much about it.

"Just this and that," I tell them.

Trudie wants to see, but I say no, it's private. I can see her disappointed look, so I tell her that if she saves her money, I will take her to the store to buy her own notebook. She likes that idea so much that she runs into our room and starts counting her pennies right then and there.

It is October. The days are getting cooler, and it gets dark earlier now. The war is still going on in Europe, and I feel sad thinking of all those poor soldiers outside in the cold. Mama's brother Lev went into the army not long ago and has not been heard from since. I've caught Mama crying sometimes, and I know this is why. I write about all of it in my notebook, and when I do, it's as though I have been carrying a heavy stone that I am finally able to set down.

Suddenly I have an idea that is so obvious, I can't believe I didn't think of it before. I will write a letter to Bernadette Louise. True she is only a doll, but that doesn't matter. I remember the notes I used to tuck in the box with her and know that this is the right thing to do.

I wait until my sisters are busy and Mama is in the kitchen cooking supper. I know she keeps paper and envelopes in a drawer in the shop, so I quietly go downstairs to take what I need. I don't think she would mind, but somehow, I don't want ask, either.

The shop looks different now. The shelves are filled with the new dolls Papa and Mama have been making, not the old ones they used to fix. But at least they are filled with something.

Then I have to do a really sneaky thing, something that makes my heart pound. I go to the oak card file where Papa keeps the names and address of his customers. I flip through the cards, just the way he did when he was writing to all those people about coming to pick up their dolls. It's easy to find the one I am looking for. He's very organized. I stare at the name and address of the woman who came and took Bernadette Louise away:

MISS PAMELA MACKAY
135 EAST 17TH STREET
NEW YORK CITY

When I take the card out of the box, my hand feels a little shaky. It's not really wrong, I tell myself. But if that's true, why do I feel so nervous? I copy the address into my notebook and put the card away. I also take two penny stamps from Papa's drawer. I make a promise to myself to leave the next two pennies I get in the drawer to repay him. Then I hear Mama calling me to set the table, so I have to hurry back upstairs.

I don't have chance to sit down and write the letter until two days later, but when I do, I know exactly what I want to say. I write it in my notebook first, so I can make any changes I need to make, and then I copy it over onto the sheet of Mama's letter paper, using my very best script. Miss Abbott gave me a gold star for my penmanship, so I can certainly be neat when I want to. This is what I write:

Dear Bernadette Louise,

I miss you! I wish you didn't have to leave the doll shop, but I know you had to go back to your real owner. I thought I was your owner because of how much I loved you, but I guess that was not true. Do you remember Angelica Grace and Victoria Marie? And Trudie and Sophie? They all miss you, too. Maybe you can come back to visit sometime. We could have a tea party again. Mama is teaching us to bake, and I will bake something for you. Remember the fun we used to have? I hope you are having fun now in your new-old home. Think of me. I will be thinking of you.

Yours always,

Anna

Then, at the bottom, I write a little note asking Miss MacKay if she will read my letter to Bernadette Louise. I worry about this part for a while. Maybe she will think I'm being silly. But writing is the first thing that has made me feel better since Bernadette Louise was taken away, so I know I have to do it. I address the envelope, and when Mama sends me to Mr. Bloom's store for parsley, I bring the letter with me. There is a mailbox right across the street, and I watch the envelope—now sealed, addressed, and stamped—slide down the blue metal chute.

Nothing happens after that. I wait—for what, I'm not sure. I don't actually think that Bernadette Louise is going to write me back, do I? Still, I can't shake the feeling that my writing to Bernadette Louise will help.

It's November now. The days get shorter, and it's turning cold. Sophie, Trudie, and I have to wear scarves, knitted hats, and coats when we walk to school. I can see my breath, white and cloudy, in the chilly, morning air. I've grown so much this past year that my old coat doesn't fit. Mama says she will give it to Trudie, and she will make me a new coat. Together, we go to a big fabric store on Orchard Street. Up a long flight of stairs, the store is a great, open room filled with bolts and bolts of fabric, all standing on end with narrow aisles in between the rows. Midnight-blue velvet, black and gold brocade, plaids and checks, silks and wools. Every kind of fabric in the world must be there. I help Mama choose the fabric for my new coat. It's dark brown wool, soft and nubby. I like it because I think it looks very grown-up. We choose black buttons and black braid for the trim. I even sew on some of the trim myself.

Maybe I am getting too old for dolls, I tell myself. Maybe I don't even want a doll anymore. But then I see Sophie playing with Victoria Marie, and I know that I will never, ever, be too old for dolls. I am just writing those very words in my notebook—and underlining them, too—when Mama calls me downstairs. I snap the book closed and tuck it into my pocket. Is there a chore I have forgotten? Or maybe she needs me to get something from Mr. Bloom's store.

When I get downstairs, I wish I could go running back up them again. There is Miss MacKay. In one hand, she holds an embroidered tapestry bag. In the other, she holds a letter. My letter—I recognize the handwriting right away. Her cane is nowhere in sight.

"Anna, Miss MacKay came back to see us," Mama says. I can't tell from her voice whether she thinks this a good thing or not.

"Nice to see you again, Anna," Miss MacKay says.

"Nice to see you, too," I mumble. Am I in trouble? I still can't tell.

"I got your letter. I read it to Bernadette Louise, just like you asked."

"You did?"

"Yes. And do you know what she said?"

"She said something?" My voice is high and squeaky. I know that dolls can't talk. Miss MacKay must know that, too. Is she making fun of me? I feel my cheeks heat up and I steal a glance at Mama. But she is smiling. And when I look back at Miss MacKay, she is smiling, too.

Cautiously, I let my breath out. It doesn't look like I'm in trouble.

"Bernadette Louise said she wanted to come back here. And live with you." Miss MacKay looks in her bag and pulls out a wrapped package and hands it to me. "You open it."

When I do, I find Bernadette Louise inside.

"You mean you're giving her to me?" I say.

"Yes, I am."

"Really and truly?" I ask.

"Really and truly," says Miss MacKay.

"But why?" I say. I still can't believe this is for real.

"Because I think this is the right home for her. I thought so when I first met you. And then when you sent the letter, I was sure."

"I did miss her," I confess. "Writing to her seemed to help."

"Writing often does," says Miss MacKay, and her gaze drifts off, as if she is thinking of something else. But then she looks at me again. "You know, I've had this doll since I was a child. She belonged to my grandmother."

"Really?"

"Yes, really. I was rather rough on her I'm afraid. And then she was misplaced for a while when I moved, and so she ended up in terrible shape. But when she came here, you made her well again."

"I loved her when she was broken, too. But I thought she would be happier being whole again," I say.

"I think that's true," says Miss MacKay. "I've been

wanting to give her to another girl—but only a girl who would play with her and love her the way you do. I hadn't found the right one—until now."

"Thank you," I say, running my fingers over Bernadette Louise's shiny black hair. "Thank you so much." Funny how I still feel like crying, only now for a very different reason.

"Yes, thank you so much," says Mama. There is a noise on the stairs, and then I see Sophie and Trudie come into the shop. They are both holding their dolls and I can see that they can't wait to find out what is happening. "Please let me introduce my other daughters. This is Sophie," Mama says. "And this is Trudie. Girls, say hello to Miss MacKay."

"Pleased to meet you," says Sophie, and then, when Sophie gives her a little nudge, Trudie says the same thing.

"You know, it's so raw out there," says Mama. "Wouldn't you like to stay and have a cup of tea with us before you go?"

"I would be delighted," says Miss MacKay, who unbuttons her coat and hands it, along with her hat, to Mama. While Mama chats with Miss MacKay, I quickly tell Trudie and Sophie what has just happened. Sophie gives me a hug while Trudie turns and pulls on the sleeve of Mama's dress.

"Can we have a tea party, Mama?" she asks. "For the dolls, too?"

"I think that's just what we should do," says Mama as she smiles down at her. We all head upstairs to the kitchen, where I help set the table while Mama brews the tea. The dolls sit at the box that is sometimes a bed and right now a table and enjoy their tea served from the special yellow tea set. Sophie, Trudie, and I tell Miss MacKay all about all the wonderful things that have happened in the doll shop downstairs. And it seems as we talk—our voices mingling, overlapping, yet each eager to be distinct and to be heard—that the most wonderful things are still to come.

# Author's Note

I've always loved dolls. I played with dolls as a child and collected them an adult. Dolls, and the little girls who love them, have been at the heart of many of my books for children. My interest in the topic led me to read about a girl named Bertha Alexander. Bertha's father, a Russian Jewish immigrant, repaired china, porcelain, and bisque. People brought him their chipped plates and cups, cracked teapots, and broken platters to fix. Since at that time, dolls were made of china, porcelain, and bisque, he fixed them, too. He established America's very first doll hospital, on the Lower East Side of New York City. The Alexander family lived in an apartment above the shop; sometimes Bertha and her sisters were allowed to go downstairs and play with the dolls that were waiting for repair. What a treat *that* must have been.

Then the First World War broke out in Europe. America didn't join in right away. But the effects were still felt by many Americans. Trading with Germany became difficult, and then impossible. In 1917, the United States government imposed an embargo on German-made products. This meant that our country would neither buy products from Germany nor sell the Germans any products that were made here. Since Germany was the world leader in doll and toy manufacturing, the doll parts needed by Bertha's father came from Germany. Once the embargo was imposed, the parts were no longer available.

Bertha, who later changed her name to Beatrice, was by this time already a grown woman, with a husband of her own. She was worried about what would happen to her parents and wanted to help them. That's when she came up with the brilliant idea of making her own dolls, dolls that didn't depend on German parts. Setting up shop on her kitchen table, she began experimenting. Thus, a doll-making empire was born. Madame Alexander dolls, with their blue and pink flowered boxes and finely tailored clothes, became known and loved by generations of girls all over the world.

This seemed to me like the perfect idea for a children's story. The characters and the details would be my own, but the setting would be taken from Beatrice's real-life experience. So *The Doll Shop Downstairs*, while fiction, has its roots in a real, historical moment. An immigrant family that made its home on the Lower East Side of New York City, a craft learned in Europe, a bevy of little girls living above a doll repair shop, a terrible war that took so many lives and caused hardship and suffering in so many others— these were the factual elements I used to weave a tale of my own. I hope that it will inspire a new generation of readers to think about those long-ago times in a fresh, sympathetic, and more immediate way.

# GLOSSARY OF TERMS

BISQUE—fine, unglazed porcelain; has a matte, or unshiny, finish

BUCKRAM—a stiff fabric of cotton or linen used for linings

CHINA—glazed porcelain; has a shiny finish

EMBARGO—a legal restriction on buying and selling goods between two countries

GLAZE—the finish put on porcelain, often very shiny

MUSLIN—a kind of coarse cotton cloth

ROSH HASHANAH—Jewish New Year

SHUL—Jewish house of worship

SKEIN—a loosely coiled length of yarn

SUKKOS—Jewish harvest festival

YOM KIPPUR—Jewish Day of Atonement; holiest day in the Jewish calendar

# TIMELINE

1870—F.A.O. Schwartz, the world-famous toy store, opens in New York City on Broadway and Ninth Street.

1860s—French bisque dolls become very popular in Europe and the United States.

1880s–1920s—German bisque dolls dominate the toy market.

1892—Ellis Island immigration station opens in New York. For millions of immigrants, this is the first stop in America. Like Anna's parents, many of these immigrants are from Russia, though they come from other countries, like Poland, Italy, Germany, Norway, and Ireland, too.

1898—Population of New York City reaches nearly 3.5 million, making it the second largest city in the world; the Lower East Side, where Anna and her family lives, is one of the most crowded neighborhoods in the world.

1904—New York City gets its first subway line; Anna's family often uses the subway, which costs five cents.

1904—The edible ice cream cone is introduced at the World's Fair in St. Louis.

1914—World War I begins in Europe.

1917—United States enters World War I.

1918—Peace treaty signed by the Allies and Germany; World War I ends.

# DISCUSSION GUIDE AND ACTIVITIES

- Which things in the story are based in fact? Which things in the story are invented?

- Historical fiction is a blend of fact and fiction. Do you think reading historical fiction is a good way to learn about history? Why or why not?

- Where do the Breittlemanns come from originally?

- Anna's family runs a doll repair shop. What other types of businesses exist in her neighborhood?

- What did you learn about Jewish customs and traditions from reading this book?

- Can you describe the apartment Anna and her family share? How does it compare with your apartment or house?

- Anna finds that writing a letter is a good way to deal with her feelings of sadness, loss, and separation. Have you ever used writing in this way? Try writing a letter to someone far away, or begin a diary or dream journal.

- Anna's family comes from Russia to the United States, but during the nineteenth and twentieth centuries, people emigrated from many other countries as well. Where did your family come from? Do you know any stories about your family's background, experiences, and culture?

Turn the page for a preview
of the next book about
Anna and her sisters . . .

*The*

*Cats*

*in the*

DOLL SHOP

# Words from Far Away

It all starts with the letters. Not that letters, all by themselves, are such an odd thing. Papa and Mama run Breittlemann's Doll Shop, where they make dolls, and they get letters all the time: from Mr. Greenfield, the buyer at the big, fancy toy store uptown called F.A.O. Schwarz, and from buyers at other stores, too. There are letters from suppliers of the different materials they use: velvet and cotton, wool and felt. Sometimes they get letters from people who have bought one of the dolls and want to know if there are any new models available.

But the letters I am talking about are different. They come all the way from Russia, where Mama and Papa were born, and they arrive in fragile envelopes that tear when they are opened. My sisters and I can't read what is in the letters, because they are written in Yiddish, which is the language both of my parents' families spoke back in what Mama calls the "old country." Sophie, my big sister, can understand Yiddish when she hears it spoken, but even she—a regular smarty-pants, all A's and gold stars at school—cannot understand the words, which are written in Hebrew letters and crowded onto the thin, pearl gray sheets of paper.

First the letters come only once in a while. Then we begin to notice that they are coming every week, sometimes even twice a week. Mama rips the envelopes in her haste to open them—did I mention they are fragile?—and all the features on her face seem to draw together, as if pulled tight by a thread, as she reads. Sometimes she looks worried long after she has finished reading the letters. Tonight is one of those times.

"What's wrong, Mama?" asks Trudie, my younger sister. It is a Sunday in August, and we're all sitting together at our small, crowded table. Dinner—cold beet soup called borscht, with dumplings and bread—is over, and I am wondering if Mama will let us go downstairs and play in the doll shop. Even though we girls are getting older—Trudie is nine, I'm eleven, and Sophie is thirteen—we still like to play with our dolls.

"Nothing's wrong," Mama says to Trudie. But the tone of her voice lets me know this is not true, and because of this, I don't ask to go downstairs after all. I decide to stay up here, so I can keep an eye on what is happening. And sure enough, after Sophie and I have finished doing the dinner dishes, Mama calls us all together in the tiny parlor that is just off the kitchen. Papa sits in his chair on one side of the room. Mama sits in her chair on the other. But instead of the sewing basket she usually brings out in the evenings, she has the letters—all of them it seems—fanned out in her lap.

"Girls, we are going to have a visitor," Mama says.

"A visitor? Who is it?" Trudie asks.

"Is it someone we know?" asks Sophie.

"Not yet," Mama says, glancing over at Papa. "But you'll get to know her soon. In fact, you'll get to know her very well."

"Tell us who it is, Mama!" Trudie pleads.

"It's your cousin Tania," Mama says.

"She's Aunt Rivka's daughter," I say. Mama has told us about her. "She and I have exactly the same birthday and we're exactly the same age. You said it was a coincidence that you and your sister both had baby girls on the very same day."

"That's right, Anna!" says Mama.

"So what's she like?" Sophie asks me, as if she didn't quite believe it when I said I remembered hearing about her.

"Well, she has blonde hair . . ." I begin. I am not actually sure about this, but when I speak again, I try to make my voice sound very confident anyway. "Long blonde hair and bright blue eyes. Blue as . . ." I have to think for a minute. "Blue as forget-me-nots."

"You've never even *seen* a forget-me-not," says Sophie. She tosses her own shining brown hair—always brushed, always neat, and always perfect—back over her shoulders.

"How do you know?" I say hotly. Sophie and I get along pretty well most of the time, but every now and then she acts like she knows everything and I know just about nothing. I don't know why it's important to me to insist that Tania is blonde and blue-eyed. Maybe it's because I know Sophie wishes she were both.

"That's enough, girls," says Mama. "Tania does have blonde hair, or at least she did when she was a baby. It might have gotten darker by now. And Rivka says her eyes are very blue. But that's not what's important right now."

"What *is* important, Mama?" Trudie asks. She is clutching her favorite doll, Angelica Grace, to her chest. "The reason she's coming here?"

"Yes, that's it," says Mama. "The reason that she's coming here." Mama puts her arm around Trudie. "You see, her papa died when she was a baby, and she has no brothers and sisters. So for a long time, it was just Rivka and Tania, living together in their little village. But now Aunt Rivka wants to move to the city. She's going to be a maid in a very fine house in Moscow."

"Isn't that a good thing?" I ask. I know about the Great War that is still going on in Europe. Papa has said that jobs are scarce, and so I would think Aunt Rivka is lucky to have found one.

"It is, except the house where Rivka will be working has no place for Tania."

"Then where will she live if she can't live with her mother?" asks Trudie. She is holding her doll and runs a finger across the smooth, painted face.

"That's exactly why she's going to come to live here," says Papa, leaning forward in his chair. "And if she lives here, she'll be able to go to school, like you girls do. She'll learn to read and write and add and subtract. That means she'll have some choices about what she wants to do when she's grown up—just like all of you."

"I'm going to be a teacher," Sophia declares.

"And I'm going to be a ballerina!" adds Trudie. Trudie does love to dance.

"You can't just decide to *be* a ballerina," Sophie says. "You have to study for a long, long time."

"Oh well," says Trudie. "So I won't be a ballerina. I'll be an actress then. Or a singer." She seems to consider the possibilities. "I know—a nurse! Just like Nurse Nora." With her jaunty little outfit and sweet, caring expression, Nurse Nora is the most popular of the dolls we make in the shop.

I can see that Sophie does not believe any of this. She has that I'm-so-grown-up look on her face. Maybe

I shouldn't even say what I want to be. Sophie will find some way to make me think it's not possible. Or that it's silly. But I decide I don't care.

"I'm going to be a writer," I announce boldly. "I'll write stories and poems and maybe even plays." Everyone turns to look at me. "My books will be published in beautiful leather-covered volumes with gold lettering on the front. People everywhere will read them. They'll be in libraries all over the city. No, all over the country."

I happen to love libraries. Once a week, I walk up to the Tompkins Square Library on Tenth Street where I can check out books. I have my very own library card. The librarian, Miss Abbott, is so nice. She sets aside things she thinks I will like. She's always right, too. What if one day Miss Abbot were able to give a book I wrote to some other little girl coming through those doors? Wouldn't I feel proud!

"Those are all fine dreams," says Mama. "If you work hard in school, you'll make them come true. And Tania— we want her to have a chance to dream, too."

"How long will she be staying?" Sophie wants to know. "Will we have enough room for her?" I have to admit these are good questions. Our apartment has only four small rooms—kitchen, parlor, and two bedrooms.

"Your mother and I have talked about that," Papa says, glancing over at Mama. From that glance, I can tell that some of the conversations haven't been so smooth. "Tania will be here with us for about a year," he continues.

"A year! That's a long time," says Sophie.

"Aunt Rivka needs that much time to make the money for her own passage," Mama says. "And then she'll come over, too, and we'll help her find an apartment of her own nearby."

"It's going to be crowded," Trudie says. Sophie nods vigorously.

"Yes," Mama says, lifting her chin a little. "It will be. And it may not be easy to have another girl living in your room."

"We'll manage," I tell Mama. "You can count on us." Sophie and Trudie don't say a thing. "When will she be here?"

"That's what Rivka and I are trying to arrange now," says Mama. "I'll let you know as soon we've figured it out."

Shortly after that conversation, September starts and with it, school. Trudie is in fourth grade now. She has the same teacher I had back when I was in that class. Sophie is in eighth grade, her last year in our school. Next year she'll be in high school, which seems impossibly grown up to me. And I'm in sixth grade, right smack in the middle, where I always am.